A SECRET PLACE OF THUNDER

THE PATRIARCHS COVENANT SERIES BOOK ONE

PATRICIA D. ADAMS

A
SECRET
PLACE OF
THUNDER
THE PATRIARCHS COVENANT SERIES
PATRICIA D. ADAMS

A Secret Place of Thunder

The Patriarchs Covenant Series Book one

Patricia Adams

Printed in the United States of America

First Printing, 2018

EISBN-13 (eBook): 978-1-7329509-0-0

ISBN-13 (paperback): 978-1-7329509-1-7

A Secret Place of Thunder

COPYRIGHT © 2018 by Patricia D. Adams

COPYRIGHT © Image and cover design by ReginaWamba.com

www.patriciadadams.com

Patricia Adams- Self Publishing

P.O. Box 5521

Alvin, Texas 77512-5521

TABLE OF CONTENTS:

CHAPTER ONE 11

CHAPTER TWO 18

CHAPTER THREE 33

CHAPTER FOUR 46

CHAPTER FIVE 56

CHAPTER SIX 65

CHAPTER SEVEN 79

CHAPTER EIGHT 92

CHAPTER NINE 102

CHAPTER TEN 113

CHAPTER ELEVEN 125

CHAPTER TWELVE 148

CHAPTER THIRTEEN 168

CHAPTER FOURTEEN 187

CHAPTER FIFTEEN 198

CHAPTER SIXTEEN 210

CHAPTER SEVENTEEN 221

CHAPTER EIGHTEEN 234

CHAPTER NINETEEN 254

CHAPTER TWENTY 264

CHAPTER TWENTY-ONE 272

CHAPTER TWENTY-TWO 279

CHAPTER TWENTY-THREE 297

CHAPTER TWENTY-FOUR 317

THE REALM OF DUALITY 341

CHAPTER ONE 343

ACKNOWLEDGEMENTS 354

For my children, after all,

a parent cannot tell their children

to reach for the stars

if they themselves do not try.

I love you!

CHAPTER ONE

I was terrified. I didn't have a clue where I was, and I couldn't remember how I got there. The air was humid and musty as the faint smell of rotting flesh and the unwavering stench of raw sewage dominated my every sense with each passing breath.

It was cold and dark and was so unnervingly quiet my chattering teeth seemed to bounce through the cave in strange, echoed patterns. Adrenaline raged in my veins. I desperately needed to move, but my body protested each slight shift. Memories and images flashed behind my closed eyes. My enemies were surrounding me as I was chased to torment.

A stone was heaved upon me as water surged over my face, and as I settled my life in the dungeon, I cried out from the darkness below, "My soul must be saved, and heartache placed against their hatred…"

I opened my eyes; I needed to find a way out, and fast. I knew I was deep in the underground bowels of the city with no real idea how to navigate the dark landscape.

When in doubt, instinct always won. My ears, acting in overdrive, picked up the faint, yet distinct, sound of voices from above me. Lifting my face toward the voices, I saw a faint circle of light. Perfect, my way is up. I thought.

Dragging myself into a sitting position, I tried to get my bearings. I felt for the wall; the rough jagged stones pricked my fingers. I felt my way around the cell and instantly knew three things: first, the room was small and square; second, the stones were going to slice my bare feet to shreds, because I was going to use them as leverage for my climb; and third, I was going to need a miracle.

Tearing off strips of fabric from my clothes, I bound my hands and feet, hoping the measly tattered cloth would provide some sort of protective barrier against the cutting, razor-sharp stones. My nails were already broken past the quick, but, really, who cared? In a few moments, I'd finally be free.

I made record time with the agonizing climb. My body was shaking with the strain and effort; I didn't have much strength left. I said a quick thank you prayer and shoved single-handedly, mustering as much strength as I could, at the boulder above. By divine intervention, the stone was rolled away.

Cloaked in silence, I scurried out of the hole and into the rarely used passageways of the castle, praying silently all the way. I passed a dark hooded cloak drying on a clothesline and grabbed it. This would have to do, I thought. It was big, but it would hide the blood and damages to my battered body. Maybe I could go unnoticed for a few more precious moments.

I continued winding through the castle keep, turning down unused and never-traversed paths. There was a bright light at the end of the tunnel just up ahead, and it wasn't the figurative kind.

There really was a light illuminating my path. I hurried toward it, fearful of the unknown people I could feel chasing me. Only a few more moments until they realized I was missing.

Shouting ensued down the street. Oh no! They'd finally realized I'd escaped, I thought, as I picked up my pace. It was too late. I would not be persecuted because of whom I follow, I thought, as I continued my awkward run toward the light, rushing as much as my broken body would let me.

As soon as I hit the blinding light, I was hurled onto a vast field and a raging battle. Battle cries echoed in my ears. Red and white, white and red, Roman soldiers fought. It was like a majestic, yet gory dance.

Some soldiers wore red tunics with a silver body armor glinting in the sun and scarlet horsehair plumes on their helmets. The red ones were throwing Javelins at the ones in white and gold.

I immediately looked down to assess my own garments; they were white and gold. The body armor was made with intricate filigree scroll work. It was heroic and oddly beautiful. The tunic was of the purest white.

The sandals that wrapped around my feet and up my calves were made of the softest leathers but were, somehow, adorned with the same metallic gold filigree scrolls.

The golden shield in my left hand was light compared to its size. A massive realistic-looking lion's head was carved into it; I'd never seen anything so beautiful. The golden sword I carried in my right hand looked more fitted to royalty. Someone called my name and snapped me out of the trance.

Acting purely on instinct, I raised my shield and blocked the javelin hurtling toward me. Another wasn't far behind. I blocked and parried any oncoming attack, and when I thought I couldn't raise my heavy sword again, I looked to the sky.

The sun glinted and threw me on top of a nearby mountain, where men still fought, red and white clashing below. But these were no longer Roman soldiers; they were the soldiers of the crusades.

No longer were the javelins being thrown about, but long broad swords were being lunged upon and thrusted. No longer were there tall, horsehair-plumed helmets, but ones carved in intricate metal work.

My lion's head shield was replaced with one that was adorned with a beautiful filigree cross. My cloak and chainmail lay heavy on my body. My white leather gloves, slicked with the blood of my enemies, looked more morbid than they should.

I realized much too late that I was not alone on this mountain. An enemy soldier silently approached. Out of the corner of my eye, I could see his studious expression. He had trained for this moment his whole life, but so had I.

I knew my enemies well, for I once called them friends. He had already drawn his sword to strike. There wasn't time to react. My sword and shield were like lead in my hands. I dropped them in the bloody snow at my feet.

I fell to my knees and raised my hands, resigned to my fate. I lifted my eyes to heaven. I made my choice. I would surrender.

I saw the sun glint a beautiful shade of gold off his polished sword. He drew his arm back in slow motion and delivered the fateful death blow. A loud crack like thunder jolted me awake.

CHAPTER TWO

"Miss Givings," pronounced a distasteful droned voice. "Would you care to join us in the land of the living today? Or would you care to visit the principal's office where you may continue your sleeping in his presence?" my history teacher, Mr. Withers, asked.

He had no idea how close to home his words were. As if on cue, the bell rang signaling the end of first period and the end of any hope of a normal first day of my junior year of high school.

I had awoken this morning with thoughts of an amazing first day of school, but as my day wore on, it became achingly clear that I wasn't just a little wrong -- I was dead wrong.

I gathered my things and darted into the hallway, escaping Mr. Withers' class as quickly as I possibly could. I ignored the snickers from the other students. I honestly hadn't meant to fall asleep in class. It was rather unusual for me to do something like that. But that didn't matter anymore. I'll just make sure I don't stay up late reading again tonight, I thought.

Pushing that aside, I smiled. I had a date with my best friend, Evie, at our usual hangout spot between classes, the soda machine. We'd met there every day since freshman year.

It was the perfect spot because it was halfway between our classes and our lockers. No one seemed to congregate around them except our small group of friends, and that was perfectly fine with us.

Evelynn Cole, or as I call her, Evie, had been my best friend since, well, practically forever. She lived three houses down from mine.

When I moved into the neighborhood at the ripe old age of five, she helped me put up flyers for a lost Boston terrier puppy we'd found roaming the neighborhood. We'd spent the whole afternoon going door to door asking about him. Finally, we gave up, and my mom let me keep him after several weeks of the flyers being up. We named him Lucky, a bit of a cliché, maybe, but, hey, we were five.

After that, we were inseparable, Lucky, Evie, and I. Some even said Evie and I were more like twins than she and her brother, Eli, who really was her twin. We didn't really look alike -- I was blonde and average and she was everything but.

She and Eli did look alike, however, from their chestnut hair, to their steel-colored eyes, to their magnetic personalities.

It was just that we loved to do the same things and laughed at the same jokes. She totally got me, and I got her.

Evie was big city, something our small town of Alvin, just wasn't. She would have fit in better living in New York or Los Angeles but not Alvin, our mostly farming community thirty miles southeast of Houston, Texas -- a place where you were more likely to spot cows and oil derricks than people and real bustling city life.

We were all pretty much considered lifers here due to the vortex that seemed to grab ahold of someone once they moved into town and never seemed to let them go. Some said this mystical force resided in the heart of our tiny town square. No one understood the draw to this place.

It was not an extraordinary town by any means, though we did have a few big-box-named stores, which, I suppose, was huge for small town. Honestly, most of us never wanted to leave. It was peaceful way out there. Which made this a running joke in our town.

Before I could meet up with Evie, I needed a trip by my locker to change out books for my next class. That was when I noticed the incident that, from then on, would forever be known as the fashion faux pas.

Abigail McClear, or Abby, as her friends called her, my arch nemesis since kindergarten, when I accidentally squirted my juice box all over the front of her frilly pink dress on picture day -- I swear it really was an accident-- walked down the hall.

At once I noticed, with horror, we were wearing the exact same dress; however, on her it was stunning. Her dress plunged where mine sagged. Her dress hit just above her knee, effortlessly showcasing her legs.

Her long white blond locks were professionally curled. The tiffany blue color of the dress brought out her amazing aquamarine eyes, which in true Abby fashion were flawlessly lined and lashed. Her heart-shaped face gave way to plump, pouty glossed lips, and her perfectly tanned dancer's legs were framed with beautiful lace peep-toe heels.

She was the kind of girl everyone noticed. Every guy wanted to date her, and every girl wanted to be her. I just wanted to curl in a ball and die with embarrassment.

I had gone shopping with my mom the week before and spotted the perfect dress for my perfect start to a perfect year of school. I spent a month's worth of allowance on it, but I had deemed it worthy. After all, anything that didn't make my five-foot, two-inch frame appear any shorter was a keeper. I had the cutest pair of sandals, and I thought the dress would look great with them.

I had dressed with care that morning, taking extra time on my fine limp, golden blonde hair, making sure it had curl that stayed. I even put on blush, mascara, and lip gloss, which, for me, was a lot of makeup.

I thought I looked polished, mature, and confident, but one look at her and I was instantly put to shame. She exuded the confidence I could only play dress up with.

Abby sashayed down the hall, her perfect clique of replicas in tow, better known as Ashley Shopel and Lindsey Abrams. Abby eyed me with annoyance. The leer she lashed out, not only told me that she too had noticed my blunder in even owning a dress like hers, but that she couldn't believe I'd embarrass her by wearing it.

Oh yeah, that, and she hated me.

I got that message loud and clear, too.

Ashley and Lindsey smirked at me, then Ashley whispered something to Lindsey and they both giggled profusely. Typical.

"Nice dress, pipsqueak," Abby growled through her teeth, disdain heavy in her posh voice. My cheeks flamed and burned. In three little words, she'd not only managed to dismiss me and insult me, but she brought the attention of every student in the jam-packed hallway our direction.

I immediately turned and as fast as I could, gathered my measly AP Biology books and shoved them into my bag. As quickly and quietly as a mouse, I escaped the hushed whispers and taunting laughs of the students nearby.

Sweet relief flooded me when I saw my exodus just down the hall. The girls' bathroom was mercifully empty. I stood in front of the mirror, shame burning my eyes and threatening to spill tears down my face. I loathed Abby McClear. No, scratch that, it was worse, I envied her.

She was queen of the school. How dare she make me feel inferior, as if I were a threat to her throne. Please. Conflicted was putting it mildly. I refused to give into the tears. I wouldn't give her the satisfaction.

I washed my face, grabbed my purple hoodie out of my bag, and pulled it on. Since my hair lay limp around my face and the remaining curl was beginning to fall, I pulled the limp locks into my go-to standard, a ponytail. I washed off most of the makeup I was wearing.

That'll do, I told my normal self, just as the final bell tolled.

Great, I sighed, now I was late to my first AP biology class of the year on top of everything else. Yeah this was totally turning out to be a perfect day. The word "perfect" should seriously be removed from my vocabulary, permanently.

"Way to go, Grace," I mumbled as I threw open the door. I ran smack dab into a solid body, which abruptly let out its own squeak of surprise.

"Hey... There you are. Where in the world have you been, missy?" She cocked her hip to the side causing her hip bone to protrude through her classic, black pencil skirt.

"I waited at our spot for like fifteen minutes, and you, my dear, were a no show. That's just rude." She pursed her pouty lips, trying to guilt trip me.

Evie was gorgeous, and quirky. She opted for the fashionable librarian look whenever she could. Today was no exception.

She was wearing a white, lace, button-up shirt with, a black satin pencil skirt and black knee-high stiletto leather boots.

Her long, curly, brown hair was twisted into a knot at the back of her head, and she had writing pens jabbed into it to hold it in place; only a few stray wisps strategically escaped.

She wore her traditional glasses, but instead of going for something subtle like most people would, she opted for red plastic frames, which were an exact contrast to her steel-colored eyes, porcelain-doll skin, and ruby-red lips.

She was every guy's fantasy; personally, I think she just liked the attention. She was valedictorian, student council president, and captain of the mathletes' club.

The girl had brains and looks. Too bad she'd chew up any prospective boyfriend material and spit him out like yesterday's lunch. She needed a mature college guy, someone who could beat her in the brainiac department and keep her on her toes. But that was my Evie for you.

"I'm sorry! I intended to be there, but..."

"It's okay, no problem; I'm just yanking your chain. By the way, did you see Abby and the replicas … uh oh, I know that look. What happened?" She stepped forward and pushed me back into the restroom.

"Abby happened," I said, trying hard not to cry. I gave her the complete rundown of the event, which shall never be spoken of again.

"Where's the queen bee now? I'd like to give her a piece of my mind." Her blushed cheeks reddened further.

"It's okay, Evie. Honestly, I just hate that I let her get to me so bad, that's all," I shamelessly admitted.

"I can't believe my brother used to date her," she said, giving voice to the thought I had had a million times.

"Oh, you know Abby is Abby; she does anything to make me feel stupid …" I paused, her words suddenly catching up to me. "… Wait, used to, what happened?" Curiosity killed the cat, and where Eli was concerned, I was curious.

"Ahhh, I see that got your attention. Well, I was planning on telling you at our spot earlier, but since we're officially skipping class now, I think we should go check out early for lunch, and I'll explain then. Off to Dairyland, my treat." She wagged her eyebrows, linked her arm through mine, and strolled, half sashaying and half dragging me out of the girls' room, down the hall to the school exit, and out to the car she shared with her brother.

Outside, the sun beat down on us. For late August, it was hot, not all that uncommon in the South. There was a saying that people had for where we lived, "There are two seasons in Texas, summer and even more summer." Honestly, I could have sworn we bordered the line to hell. Sweat was already beginning to bead on my forehead.

My stomach suddenly had butterflies, and it wasn't because this was the first illegal thing I'd ever done, even though it was.

Nope, it was because of the boy waiting by the back of a 1969 navy blue Mach1 Mustang, casually flipping through a sports magazine, as if he had no cares in the world.

Eli was the hottest boy in school; you could ask any girl. His shaggy-styled mocha hair, tall, athletic build, and cocky attitude were just a few things that did all the girls in.

For me it was the small things—the way he laughed; the uncanny way he turned everything into a joke; the love he had for his sister; how, when he thought no one was looking, he turned all serious and thoughtful; and the way his lips tilted up as his dimples appeared and those little creases at the corners of his eyes showed up when he smiled. Maybe it was the way he looked at me as though I were important. Whatever it was, I had it bad.

He was smart and athletic, but he'd rather people notice the athleticism and not the brains, often opting to keep quiet instead of answering questions that would make him sound intelligent. He was sarcastic and witty, which was yet another thing that made him so popular.

Today, however, he looked at me and cocked an eyebrow, a smirk playing on his lips, as he eyed me up and down from behind the magazine. I sighed, knowing I was about to have to take a ribbing.

Sometimes his jokes were infuriating and embarrassing. He had a way of knowing which of your insecurities to flaunt and at which precise moment it would make the greatest impact. But it didn't mean he wasn't great eye candy, or that he couldn't make me laugh until I cried, and my sides hurt with the effort.

Logically, I knew we'd never make a great couple; we were opposites, like Freddie and Velma. But that didn't stop me from fantasizing or from Evie being pushy. She wanted me to be her sister, in the most real sense, and the only way that was going to happen was if I married her only brother. Ha, fantasize much, Evie?

Eli looked up, piercing me with his steel gray eyes. "Hey, baby sis, oh and...uh...hello to you, pipsqueak." Obviously, he felt proud of his sense of humor because he was stifling a smile, completely unsuccessfully I might add.

"Yeah, yeah," I rolled my eyes, "Laugh it up, lover boy. You're just jealous she thought of it first."

"Nice dress," he retorted snickering, no longer able to control his bubbling laughter. His humor escaped me. Keep laughing, I thought.

"At least I didn't date the queen bee." The thought escaped my mouth before I could reign it in. I giggled, his laughter catching me.

"Oh, don't even go there right now!" Evie exclaimed, saving me from being catty, and slapping his arm for good measure.

"Ouch! Didn't your momma teach you better manners, sis?" he joked, rubbing at the reddening spot on his arm.

"You would know; she's your momma, too!" Evie retorted, rolling her eyes.

"So, I'm getting the hungry vibe, and it feels like a tortilla burger kind of day; am I close?" he asked, trying to change the subject so he wouldn't get into more trouble with Evie.

"Right on both accounts as usual, bro." She sounded shocked, but she shouldn't have been. This had been an ongoing game with the two of them for as long as I had known them.

"Gosh, sometimes, you guys take the whole twin thing to extremes."

I sighed, shook my head, and stepped around the twins. I somehow managed to finagle myself gracefully into the back seat without tripping and or exposing my backside. Yay, bonus points for me!

I leaned out the window and yelled, "Hey, are we leaving or what?"

"Coming, princess," they chimed in unison.

CHAPTER THREE

Dairyland was unlike any other restaurant in town. When you turned into the parking area you pulled off a paved street and directly onto a gravel parking area.

Small but efficient, it essentially consisted of a small metal building which served as its kitchen and its service counter. It had a wraparound carport and a covered picnic area reserved for dine-in guests, though dining in wasn't truly in a building; it was picnicking under a covered area.

When looking at this building it at first appeared old, like that of the 50s-style drive-in building, homage to its heritage and era of the original 1960s restaurant.

Dairyland had served generations of our local patrons for over fifty years, outlasting even some of the more modern and chain restaurants. It was the kind of place people wouldn't think twice about stopping into. Its' delicious reputation was like a secret only we who'd lived here knew.

You really couldn't go wrong ordering anything from the menu since it was all cooked fresh to order. However, since we were "home towners", Dairyland's tortilla burger had become a staple for our meals, rather than what most people regularly ate at fast food chains.

Dairyland was home to the original Tortilla Burger. Tortilla Burgers were made from two corn tortillas fried until crisp, with a flame-grilled hamburger pattie and melted American cheese. Add on fresh lettuce and tomato, onion and pickled jalapeño—or, in my case, mild, with no onions and no jalapeño—and you had yourself a Tortilla Burger. Of course, Dairyland served other fast comfort foods, but, honestly, the Tortilla Burger was what everyone went there for.

Most of the time, Dairyland stood empty, but today there were two other cars full of people parked under the awning eating their food. Eli put the car in park in one of the spots and hopped out.

"You ladies want the usual?"

"Yes, for me," yelled Evie.

"Yes, please," I uttered, trying not to drool.

Eli nodded and walked toward Beatrice, the chubby grandmotherly lady—well if your grandmother smoked for fifty-plus years and had an over-hair-sprayed, silver bouffant hairdo, that is—at the order window, while Evie and I walked wordlessly to the back table.

I personally thought Eli liked to order because Beatrice had a soft spot for him. She usually upsized our drinks free when he ordered. He flirted with everyone.

"So now that he's a single man again, when are you going to make your move?" Evie asked as she slid into the picnic table and nudged me with her elbow at the same time.

"I have no idea what you're talking about," blushing as I replied.

"Yeah, okay, we'll do it your way." She took a deep breath and just couldn't help herself. "You know you both like each other; it's written on both of y'alls faces when each of you isn't looking, but I'm looking. I don't see why you guys can't just go on a date and get it over with. Besides, I've told you both time and time again you are going to be my sister for real one day, and the sooner you both acknowledge that the quicker it'll happen..."

"Evie, hush," I interrupted.

"But I wasn't finished..."

"Evie!" I yelled just as Eli approached the table.

"So, what are you two gabbing about over here?" He passed us our drinks and straws.

"Nothing," Evie answered, while I just sipped my Coke. I figured if I had my mouth full, I didn't have to answer, so, I was going to keep my mouth full.

"Yeah, mm hmm, right, and that's why Grace looks like she just walked a mile on the surface of the sun." He took a drink and seemed to consider whom he was talking to. "You know what, on second thought, I really don't want to know."

Just as he was about to slide into his side of the table, Beatrice announced over the intercom, in her thick twangy graveled voice, that our food was ready.

The rest of lunch was uneventful. We chatted about our schedules. It turned out that I had Eli and Evie each in one of my other classes, which having Evie in Trigonometry would be awesome, but I'd dreaded the torment from Eli in Biology. We talked until it was time to throw our trash away and hit the next class period. All in all, it was an excellent lunch and an even better distraction from the morning's events.

The rest of my day passed in a blur. Nothing out of the ordinary happened, and I managed not to fall asleep or see Abby again before the final bell. Evie had texted me to tell me she was staying after school, that she'd call later, and that I should find Eli and get him to take me home. But after one look at Eli, locked in a majorly heated conversation with Abby, I decided that maybe I should walk home after all.

The way Eli and Abby were looking at each other it was apparent they were an item again. That shouldn't have surprised me, but it kind of did. It also shouldn't upset me, but it did.

I couldn't help the pang of jealousy and the feeling of loss. It wasn't like he was mine, but in a way, he had always felt like mine, even when he was annoying and picked on me.

Evie had told me on our way to class after lunch that the reason Eli and Abby had broken up was because he caught her flirting with other guys. I mean, how could she flirt with anyone else when she had the attention of the one boy I'd gladly accept. I didn't know a lot about relationships, but it seemed weird to me.

They were just too different. He was nice, and she wasn't. But in the world of high school they made perfect sense—the classic jock and cheerleader pair. Differences or not, they were an item more often than not.

"Grace!" Eli yelled running up and grabbing my bag from me. "Evie's staying after school; she said to take you home. You ready to go?"

"Uh, it's okay, Eli; I'll just walk; it's not far." I tried to shrug him off and take my backpack back from him, but he wouldn't let go.

"Walk? Why on earth would you do a thing like that when I have a perfectly good car to take you home in?" he quizzed. If there was anything that drove me crazy it was Eli's persistence in being a pain in my rear end.

"Well, for starters, I could always use the exercise, and, second, I'm sure you and Abby have plans." I moved once again to take my stuff back, and this time I was successful in wrenching my bag out of his hands. I winced at the way that sounded, like a jaded ex-girlfriend—a sound I had no reason to make, much less a right.

"Ah, so that's what this is about; you saw that, huh?" He sounded genuinely disappointed. Poor fella... yeah. "She keeps trying to convince me to get back with her. I just can't. She's not the same, I'm not the same, and it was fun hanging out with her for a while, but no thanks." He tried to shrug it off as no big deal, but the disgusting images were burned on my retinas forever.

Abby's public display of her Eli relationship was a huge deal. No girl would be able to go near him without the rumors spreading like a stomach bug.

He wrestled my backpack away from me again, slung an arm around my shoulder, and walked me out to his car. "Besides, if I was still interested in her, I wouldn't be here to bug you, now would I?"

I caught a glimpse of Abby down the hall still standing where he'd left her, and if she didn't hate me enough before, she surely did now. Oh boy, I suppose that meant it was my turn with the plague, as if I didn't have enough social anxiety to deal with, thanks to Abby.

"So, you have a birthday coming up, any plans?" I'm not sure if he asked for genuine curiosity or if he was probing to see if I knew anything about the plans Mom and Evie had been making for months now.

"None that I'm aware of, but you know how Mom is; if she can surprise you, then you're going to be surprised." I relented.

I was pretty sure most of my birthday parties had been surprise parties. My mom had a thing about surprises, and me, well I hated them. Weird, I know, yet true, all the same.

It all started a long time ago when my mom tried to surprise me with a singing clown at my fourth birthday party. The clown came, the clown sang, I ran screaming, and cried for a solid hour. I refused to come out of my room to open presents and eat cake. I have hated so-called surprises since. Whatever the shenanigans my mom was up to this year, I'd grin and bear it for her sake.

That was all that was spoken on the ride home. There were ten whole minutes of silence, with both of us far away in our own minds. I didn't usually mind silence, but with Eli it just felt awkward. Here sat a boy who was, let's face it, pretty much like my good-looking older brother figure, one who knew everything there was to know about me.

There were no secrets between us, yet we didn't even know what to say to each other when we were alone. He pulled up in my driveway and I hopped out, hoping to escape any further awkwardness.

"Thanks for the ride." I grabbed my bag from the floor and turned to wave.

"You're welcome," he called as I shut the door. He leaned over the passenger seat, quickly rolled the window down, and paused a moment, conflict warred on his face. I could tell something was bothering him, but he didn't know if he should tell me or not.

"Hey, Grace, you looked really nice today. I'm sorry Abby was so mean to you." He rolled the window up, pulled out of the drive, and left me standing there with my mouth agape. How was I supposed to respond to that? Did he mean it? Or was he just picking on me like he usually did?

Finally, I managed a more coherent thought and turned to check the mail. All bills. Great. Mom worked loads of overtime but never managed to pay a single bill on time.

Don't get me wrong, I loved my mom; she worked hard to provide the necessities for us to live. It was just that I was left alone quite a bit.

My mom didn't date often—okay, more like never. I couldn't remember a single date she had ever been on. She didn't talk about what happened to my dad, so I assumed horrible scenarios that had left her too badly scarred to date. I had heard horror stories about parents dating, though, so I considered myself lucky.

My mom was elegant and poised; I guess I got my clumsy awkwardness from my dad. Oh, sure, I had my mom's golden blonde hair and green eyes—most people said I was her mini me—but she was so polished and regal it really didn't seem fair. She must have been a beauty queen or a debutante in her past. Again, not something she talked a whole lot about.

I had learned to quit asking about grandparents, aunts, and uncles; she'd only tell me that sometimes in order to move forward with your life, there were some people you had to leave in your past.

As you can imagine, creating family trees, bring-your-dad-to-school days, breakfast with Grandma, and any "family" type event had been difficult for me growing up; but, as I had gotten older, it had become easier to ignore and to cope with.

I unlocked the front door, stopping to pet the over-zealous Boston terrier yipping at my feet. After being licked half to death and feeding Lucky, I went to start my own dinner.

I learned how to cook at a pretty young age. Mom, being a single mom for most of my life, rarely had time to cook. So as soon as I was tall enough to reach the appliances and dishes, I had cooked dinner.

That was when I found Mom's note and a twenty-dollar bill on the refrigerator door.

Grace,

I wanted you to know that I wouldn't be making it home for dinner tonight. The hospital called and asked if I would work a double shift. I know you hate it when I work nights, but we need the money. There's money for pizza, enough for Eli and Evie too. I love you baby! See you in the morning before school.

Love, Mom

She's working late again, I sighed. Okay, it was weird, but not terribly unexpected, bills and what not. I locked all the doors and turned on the porch light. I figured I'd text Evie later and started my homework

CHAPTER FOUR

Somewhere between 3:00 p.m. and the next morning, I found myself standing on a cliff's edge watching a storm's approach.

For whatever reason, I had never understood my attraction to approaching storms. The preceding breeze blew my moss-green, gauzy gown against my legs, the air a cool caress against my skin.

My yearning heart awaited the majestic sounds of other approaching hearts and beating wings. As always, the anticipation lingered until the dark sky filled the fleeting blue with a vast rhythm of earth-shattering thunder, and lightning streaking across the sky.

I turned my face toward the encroaching storm but in an instant was hindered by a single drop of rain to my cheek. Strange, it wasn't cool like the breeze, but warm. As I opened my eyes, I could see another approaching drop of crimson rain fleeing to the earth as if to surrender.

The sticky drops began to pound their own cadence on the earth. Before long, the valley that surrounded me was filled with blood, and still the sky flooded the earth.

I waited with bated breath; I could run no more. Soldiers slicked with red grabbed me and pulled me away, I fought and kicked, but, in the end, I was just a woman and they were men stronger than I.

There was a mock trial and I was condemned, a blasphemer, a follower of the Almighty, not the King Herod of Judea. I would never bow to a false king among men.

My death would mark the start of many in my Lord's name. But I wouldn't lose hope; the Christ child would come whether Herod believed me or not. He would come, and he would rule the earth. And in the end, they would all look like fools. After all, I was just the messenger.

I was caned and whipped with cat o' nine tails and with whips of leather and horse hide. When I could no longer stand, and their vicious and violent pleasures were had, I was viewed no more a threat and not long for this world.

They then took me to the cavern in the mountain where they threw the carcasses of the poor innocents who had been slaughtered for Harrod's selfishness, my own flesh and blood amongst them. The rotting stench was unbearable, but they sealed me in the tomb anyway.

Though I wanted nothing more than to curl in a ball and surrender to the siren's call and die a peaceful death, I prayed fervently.

"Get up my child; you'll find no rest here," a voice uttered.

I sat up, my bones weary and my body badly battered. I needed to escape. Voices drifted down to me from far above. Up, I needed to go up. I tore at my dress to cover my hands and feet and prepared my broken body for the climb.

Miracles abounded as the stone rolled away. I climbed to my feet making as hasty a retreat as I could muster.

I wound through the labyrinth that was the castle walls, turning and turning creating as much chaos in my wake to prolong another capture. I pulled the cloak I'd found around me tighter and headed for the light with steadfast determination. I was always told that you see a light when you die; I'd hoped this wasn't what they meant.

"Go forth; there is much yet to see," the voice prompted.

I closed my eyes for what seemed to be no more than a second. When I opened them, I no longer was standing amidst castle walls; instead, a rolling meadow lay before me. My body was no longer broken, and my attire had changed.

I was a soldier in the Roman army. A battle warred around me, a vast contrast to the beautiful landscape that surrounded me. My own opponent was dead beneath my feet.

Men fought all around as far as I could see. Javelins and swords clashed and clanged. Chariots and horses that had fallen lay flung about. Bodies were strewn across the meadow, warping its beauty with death. The flowers that once bloomed there withered and died before my eyes. The field transformed from something of such pure radiance to desolate and barren land.

I couldn't feel triumphant, though I knew my side had won the war. Those were my brothers and the brothers of my men at my feet. Such loss settled heavy in my stomach. How could this destruction be good? How could I call these deaths just?

"You, my warrior, fight the good fight. Be at peace. Hurry, you must push forward through this journey." Peace radiated from within me when the voice spoke.

Once more I closed my eyes and was transported on top of a mountain. A knight of the fallen stood before me. He was frozen mid-strike, as if he were in a video on pause. I knew what would soon happen to me when the scene un-paused. I'd seen this before. I would die here.

"Please, don't make me watch this again. Please!" I begged. Sobbing, I wiped my eyes and fell to my knees. "Why must I bear this witness? Why must I see this death?" I refused to watch these final moments again, so I closed my eyes to shield my sight.

"Be strong, my Grace." White light blinded me to the scene. I felt large hands grab my shoulders, much as a father would comfort his crying child.

"Awaken, Grace. Awaken and claim your throne, for my kingdom is yours." He placed his hand between my shoulders, and where he touched, I felt a tiny tingle. Once again, I knelt before him as Grace Noel Givings.

I raised my eyes to look upon my Savior. His erethreal beauty was beyond my fragile comprehension. His smile was radiant. His garments and robes were made of the purest white. His beard was long and silvery. His hair was peppered with the purest platinum color, as if it were truly made of metal. His eyes were the color of the moon at its fullest. And his smile was warm and comforting.

He was grandfatherly and beautiful. He radiated light as if the sun lived within him. He moved as if he weighed nothing, silent upon approach.

He was standing in a field of wispy clouds that rolled and lapped at his feet. The sky had turned empty and white, a nothingness, and yet everything seemed to encompass the space. The feeling in the air was one of ancient and tangible knowledge, more so than my mind would ever comprehend.

"Am I dead?" I asked him, when I finally found my voice and could speak.

He laughed a deep belly laugh and thumbed away the tears from my cheeks.

"No, you are not dead. Dear Grace, you are only just beginning to truly live. You are one of my flock, a guardian heart, a warrior, a queen amongst men. You are my consuming fire."

"I'm confused; if I am not dead, how am I here?" I gestured to the all-encompassing enclosure.

"Ah, yes that is the question, now isn't it?" He seemed to think heavily about his response.

Emotions and expressions passed across his face so quickly that I couldn't read them, and then he pulled me to my feet, cupped my face, and declared matter-of-factly, "Your blood remembers who you were and who you are. It's time to begin. You have been called upon for service. It is your duty."

He kissed my forehead and whispered, "Awaken and remember."

I opened my bleary eyes, sluggish from sleep. My dreams were becoming all too real. I could still feel the tingle between my shoulders where he placed his hand and the press of God's kiss on my brow, his words on repeat in my thoughts.

My neck hurt; apparently, sleeping on your desk at home was just as uncomfortable as sleeping on your desk at school.

Mom knocked on my door and pushed it open; Lucky looked up from his perch on my bed and yawned. Dang spoiled pup, at least one of us used the bed last night. I guess I should at least be thankful I had changed into a tank top and PJ shorts before I started my homework.

"Hey, honey you awake for school?" Her eyes seemed to take in the scene before her. "Did you sleep there all night?" Then at once her face distorted into a fearful grimace. "When did the dreams start, Grace?"

Oh no! I knew that tone. That was the first, middle, and last name voice. The voice that said I was in trouble. Really big trouble... Great.

At this point I still hadn't managed to fully wake up, yet there was something nagging and tugging at my memory; but I couldn't, for the life of me, figure out what it was. I was way too tired, in desperate need of a shower, and completely confused by my mom's befuddled expression.

I wrinkled my nose and squinted at her trying to clear the sleep from my eyes. Her face roamed my features, and her fingers reached to touch my back, where it still tingled. At once, I was overwhelmed by my mother's beauty, thinking she could have been a model.

"What's wrong with dreaming?" I asked. "It's not that big of a deal." A look of pure horror crossed my mom's face. I hurried to make the situation lighter.

"They're intense but not nightmarish. Did I yell or something? This one was worse than the first couple of times, but it's always the same dream. Really no biggie. I'm used to it now and I know how it turns out." I shrugged

Her face contorted further. Okay, that was making it worse; I guess I had a bad case of diarrhea of the mouth.

"Grace, look at me, honey, when? When did they start?" She placed her steamy coffee mug down on the desk then sat on the bed across from me, bringing us face to face. Her eyes were pleading for me to tell her she was wrong. She knew about the dreams?

"Three days ago." I tried to play it off like it was no big deal. She lowered her head and cast her eyes to the floor, looking crestfallen. I had never seen my mom so deflated.

"So, it has begun," she closed her eyes and whispered.

I watched as a single tear escaped her lashes and glistened as it fell down her cheek. She was truly afraid.

CHAPTER FIVE

"Honey, we need to talk," she wiped away the tiny tear. Five little words I dreaded my mother ever saying. Yet there they were. And there she had said them. My mom was ever the queen of composure when she wanted to be, but her frailty in this seemed dooming.

"About what?" Curiosity always did get the best of me.

"Not now, later today, after school maybe. I'll call in and take off at the hospital for tonight. I'm sure Janice, or someone down there, can take care of things; there are some things that are just more important."

Whatever it was she wanted to talk about must have been big for her to be this worried and take off work. Mom never did that, either of those things.

I guess I let a worried look cross my face, or my mom just knew me that well, because she stood and picked up her coffee mug, took a sip to steady herself, and brushed the hair back from my face with her free hand.

She cupped my chin to look up at her. "No worries, sweetie. We'll talk later. Everything's okay. You'll see. Now get dressed or you're going to be late for school."

Right before kissing me on the forehead and walking out of my bedroom with Lucky following behind her. The little traitor. You could tell her heart wasn't in it. She didn't believe the situation would be okay. Could my mother act any weirder?

The rest of my morning ritual was rushed. I brushed my teeth in a blur, hurried through my simple makeup routine, pulled my hair into a ponytail, threw on jeans, and a purple t-shirt. My tennis shoes and old faithful hoodie weren't far behind.

The only reminder of the previous night was the tingle between my shoulder blades. It was intense but not painful. I hoped it would go away as the day wore on.

Rushing down the stairs, I grabbed a Pop Tart and a bottle of water from the kitchen and picked up my backpack off the counter, all just in time for the honk of the blue beast waiting outside.

"Bye, Mom," I yelled as I shut the door. Mom replied but I couldn't tell what she had said. I was in too much of a hurry.

Eli had been known to leave if he even suspected he might be late for school. Evie had been the victim of that charade once or twice. It appeared she was the victim again.

"Hey, where's Evie?" I asked Eli as I shut the creaky old car door.

"Well, good morning to you, too, sunshine." He looked at me from the corner of his eye. "Don't I get a good morning kiss?" That earned him a well-deserved and hard smack to the arm.

"Seriously, way too early for your shenanigans." I rolled my eyes. "Besides, my name isn't Abby," I cooed, as I broke a piece of my cherry Pop Tart off and popped it in my mouth.

He just laughed and rubbed his arm. "I guess someone didn't get their morning caffeine fix. Need to stop by and grab some before school?"

I sighed, "Yes, please. Mom was acting all weird this morning. She said that we need to 'talk'. She even used the 'I'm in trouble voice'. I don't even know what I did this time." And, of course, to show just how bad it was, I did the little air quotes that went with it.

"Maybe the school called for you having skipped class yesterday."

"Oh great, I didn't even think about that." I groaned and flopped back in the seat. "She's going to kill me; no, strike that, she's going to kill me and resurrect my ghost, and then lock me in a dungeon so that I can't escape to haunt anyone. Ever."

"Well, if you're a ghost, can't you just walk through the walls?" He asked playing along.

"Ever the optimist." I shook my head. "No, my mom is probably online, as we speak, looking for ways to trap a ghost in a dungeon."

"Well, let's hypothetically say your mom does kill you and turn you into a ghost, and then she does find a way to trap you in a dungeon, when she manages to find one in this part of the country that is, Evie and I will have to find a way to bust you out. It's our friend duties."

"Aw, I love you guys."

That earned me a trademark smile, one of the ones that made my tummy do funny things and my insides go all gooey.

He pulled into the convenience store parking lot, ran inside, and grabbed me a coffee. Sometimes it really did pay to have great friends.

Once at school, Eli left with a wave. Evie met me in the hall on the way to first period. Mr. Withers was really going to love me if I was late today.

"Hey." I giggled as I bumped her hip with mine. "Where were you this morning?"

"Oh, uh, I had to come set up for the pep rally early this morning. You know, student body president and all that jazz."

"Oh, come on, Evie, if I didn't know you any better, I'd say that was a ploy to get your brother and me alone." Her cheeks reddened.

"OH-EM-GEE, Evie that's unbelievable. Bad best friend, bad." I squealed and then huffed away, leaving her standing in the hallway.

"Okay, I'll give it a rest." she ran after me to catch up.

I gave her a pointed look. Evie give up? There was a better chance of getting hell to freeze over.

She raised her hands to surrender. "Really, I give up; you two are just as stubborn as ever!"

"You promise?" I pleaded.

"Promise." She exclaimed, mock waiving a white flag. As if that made it more believable.

"Let me see both hands, and toes; no crossing while you say it!" I joked back not believing her one bit where this was concerned.

She laughed and shook her head. "I promise. See ya after class, okay? You can continue your interrogation then."

I waved and walked into first period history. I took my seat just as the bell tolled.

Mr. Withers was in rare form. His monotonous voice went on and on and on about the start of the Revolutionary War, and I caught more than one person trying to fall asleep during class. I yawned, just as my phone buzzed signaling a text.

Hiding it from plain sight, I read the forwarded message.

Evie: Ugh, Abby is at it again.

Eli: Do I really want to know?

Evie: As your sister, it's my duty to inform you that the whole school thinks you and Grace are together.

Eli: Together?

Evie: Yes, together! As in BF/GF together!

Eli: So. Who cares? Just let them think whatever they want.

Evie: Are you together?"

Evie: Eli, answer me!

Evie: Just wait until lunch. I am not going to let this go.

Evie, to me, alone: Well, are you? Because he's not stopping it."

Me: So, it doesn't mean anything. It's just a rumor.

Evie: He likes you, Grace; he's not denying it!

Me: Got to go, talk to you at lunch.

Evie: Chicken.

Me: Liar. ;)

Putting the phone away, I caught myself smiling like an idiot, but the smile melted right off my face when I realized that in just a few short periods I had biology and who I shared that class with. Eli would be there. What were people going to think? How would he act? This was getting so awkward. My stomach began to bubble as a knot of nerves filled it and sank like a boulder thrown into the ocean.

CHAPTER SIX

I hurriedly walked into Mrs. Gilmore's fourth period biology class, found the furthest lab table from the front, and busied myself with my nose in a book, thinking that if Eli showed up, I would be hard to spot. I couldn't concentrate on the book, though, and that pretty much made it a pointless prop.

It didn't work. I felt his eyes bearing down on me the moment he walked in the door. What did he have, some sort of Grace radar? His silvery eyes locked with mine, and I watched as he prowled his way to the back table and, of course, the chair right next to me.

I felt his hands on the back of my chair as he slid past me to take the seat next to me, his fingers lightly brushing across my back and the spot that was still there. I winced as a jolt of lightning shot down my back. I should have thought about what an empty seat next to me might signal.

"Wow, I didn't know that I was so horrible. I can find another seat if you want." He looked saddened and disappointed, and I instantly felt guilty for avoiding him. It wasn't really his fault my inner crush on him was fully alive and aware of his cologne and closeness.

I flashed him wide eyes. I wanted to tell him that he was dreamy that he wasn't horrible at all; instead, what came out of my mouth was "No, I'm sorry it isn't that. I did something to my back and it hurts." I was trying, and failing, to sound nonchalant about everything. Honestly, the spot felt like it had been burned; it was raw and tender.

Just about that time, Abby walked in and took a seat at a table diagonally from us, Lindsey not far behind. I still wasn't sure how she managed to get one of her "replicas" in every class; it just didn't seem fair.

Abby looked around the room searching for someone—three guesses as for whom she was searching. I'd place money on Mr. Tall, Dark, and Handsome, next to me.

Lindsey leaned in and whispered to Abby, and they both cackled viciously. Obviously, Eli and I were fueling their rumors, and they found it hilarious. I, however, did not.

Eli decided to play the knight in shining armor. He leaned toward me and brushed my bangs that had escaped my ponytail behind my ear. "Where are we going Friday night?"

I couldn't help the baffled grimace my face made. "Friday?" What in the world was he talking about? Apparently, in my haste to avoid him and bury my nose unsuccessfully in a book, I'd missed a poignant conversation somewhere.

"Yeah, where am I taking you on our first date Friday?" he asked, annunciating every word loudly. I caught on quickly. This wasn't a real date, this was a make-Abby-jealous moment. Okay, I could play this part.

"Wherever you want to go. I'm not picky. Anywhere with you would be perfect." I made a little pouty face and blinked a lot, trying to mimic the look Abby used to always give him.

I guess I looked more like a baboon eating a banana because I could see he was trying extremely hard not to laugh. I suppose I hadn't yet mastered the art of flirtation. Obviously, I needed more googley-eye classes.

"Okay, pookie, I'll make sure it's the very best for you." He tapped the tip of my nose. My face went blank, and I glared at his nickname for me. Pookie. Oh, we were so going to have a conversation about that later.

He leaned back and put his arm possessively across the back of my chair, and though I knew he was just pretending to like me, I couldn't help but feel the butterflies in my stomach take flight. A girl could get used to this. I had to have drifted off to dreamland and landed smack dab into fantasy land.

Abby sat absolutely dumbfounded. I kind of felt bad for her. Okay, not really, but to be so completely dissed had to be new for her.

Lucas Bracken and Oliver Mathis walked in together and both took the seats in front of us. "'S up, Guys?" Lucas turned all bright-smiled, a knowing look crossed his face.

Lucas and Oliver were the final puzzle pieces that made up our little group. Lucas was Eli's best buddy, possibly longer than Evie and me, though that fueled constant debates in and of itself.

Evie and Oliver had quite the love-hate relationship themselves. It was quite funny to watch them assault each other with words about how superior each of their intelligence was when compared to the other.

Oliver was ranked number two in our graduating class, just behind Evie. And she never let him forget.

Oliver was kind of short for a guy, not that he wasn't taller than I was, because he was. It was just that he was shorter than most of the other boys in class. He had a geek, chic look about him. He always wore jeans and a whacky-printed button-up shirt done to the very top button, and converse sneakers in varied colors.

Today's were lime green to match the hot-pink, sunglass-wearing flamingos on his shirt. His glasses were gold wire-framed and looked like they belonged to a mature grandpa—

not a high school student—and he had a mop of wiry black hair.

His dad was from Nigeria, and his mother was from The Philippines. Oliver's heritage made him very striking and unique. He had a bright and funny personality. He was artsy instead of athletic. He could sing, dance and act, but his favorite thing was telling jokes. All in all, he definitely stood out in a crowd.

Lucas was like a shooting star. He was very bright with his blonde hair and golden highlights to his baby-blue eyes and surfer's tan. Oh, he wasn't Eli, but he was good looking by his own rights. Lucas was the star quarterback with all long and lanky muscles. And he was dating Ashley Shopel. Gag me, please! His smile was a lady-killer, flashing pearl-white teeth. He was always super nice to me. But rumor had it he was quite a flirty ladies' man.

"'S up, man?" Eli asked and without taking his arm off the back of my chair, he did some sort of complicated boy handshake with his other.

And in walked Mrs. Gilmore. "Okay, class, as I said yesterday, these are your lab partners for the remainder of the year." She absently gestured to the adjoining seats at each table. "Today we are going outside to find five things to observe under the microscope for tomorrow's assignment. Please stay with your lab partner, and you cannot go past Building D." She glanced up and took a mental note of who all was there and proceeded to dismiss us.

We made it outside and quickly collected our five things. Afterwards, I watched Eli and Lucas toss a football back and forth for a little while. They both looked as if they could play for the pros. The ball smacked with an audible thump each time the other caught it.

One particularly hard thump, left Eli with a stinging palm. He shook his hand out and yelled, "Ouch man, that's one heck of a throw!"

"Aw, did that hurt?" Lucas chided playfully. Looking around he gestured. "We need help here; can someone call the waah-mbulance?"

At that comment, they began a game of witty banter. I decided I'd leave them to it and got up to go and grab my book from inside, bringing along our collected items in the little plastic baggie.

The day had turned out to be beautiful and warm. The leaves were beginning their fall transition from green to orange and copper. There was a slight breeze to the air, and it felt good just to be outside.

On my way, I noticed a poor trampled butterfly on the ground. I had no idea what I would do with him, but I thought maybe Mrs. Gilmore would know. One of his wings was just hanging by a thread. His orange coloring was turning paler by the second. It didn't seem that he had much life left.

I never saw Eli sneak by me I only noticed him leaning casually against the doorframe. Just the shear dark mass of him was enough to block me from my intended path.

"Hey, what do you have there?" Eli asked.

I thrusted my cupped palm forward and huffed with a frown. I had never been one who liked to be snuck up on, surprises and all that jazz. "A poor little butterfly with a hurt wing; and if you'll please move, I'm going to put him in a cup."

He raised his eyebrows, clearly amused at my tone. "Hum, I don't know, pookie, maybe we should just put him out of his misery."

I glared at him. "About that. Pookie? Really?" I huffed. Now he was just being annoying.

He laughed then raised his hand as if he were going to swat the poor butterfly.

"Nooo." I exclaimed, as I protectively moved my outstretched hands away from the impending blow. "We aren't going to do anything. However, I, am going to put him in a cup and take care of him."

I opened my palm, peeking inside. "It's okay, Mr. Butterfly, the big meanie head won't hurt you, I promise."

Eli laughed, obviously intrigued. "Meanie head?"

I moved to try and go around him, but he, not so subtly, blocked my path even more.

"Meanie head is better than pookie." As I moved, the butterfly caught a gust of wind and flapped his broken wings. I frowned and thought mostly to myself, I wish he'd quit flapping so much; he's going to damage his wings even more.

Eli snorted, "Yeah, I mean, who does he think he is? He acts like he could fly earlier today or something. Stupid butterwalks." I glared at Eli and rolled my eyes.

The butterfly really began flopping in my hand, and I could feel a strange burning sensation building from my elbow to my fingertips. I was glowing. My arm was lit up like a Christmas light strand. Eli reached for my hands and as his fingers skimmed mine, I felt an electric shock rock my body. He jumped back rubbing his hands and looked at me quizzically.

I opened my cupped hand to look; as I did, the butterfly took flight. It was majestic. The butterfly seemed to glow a strange golden color leaving a trail of light dusting and glittering on the air in his path. Both Eli and I were watching it fade from sight in the sky.

"What just happened?" he asked me accusatory, awe clear on his face.

"What do you mean?" I bent down and began gathering the items we had collected for our project tomorrow. Denial was my friend.

"You happened! You shocked me!" He paused wide-eyed. "You were glowing!" He shook his head as if to deny what he had seen. That was a human standard, deny the impossible, and define the undefinable. "It has to be that jolting personality you have there," he joked.

I rolled my eyes and mock laughed, "Ha, Ha, you think you're funny, don't you?" I huffed angrily. Really, who did he think he was? I didn't do anything. It was a miracle. "The butterfly just wasn't broken like I originally thought. That's all. Okay?" I stared at my hands; they didn't look different, but the tingle of the shock was still there.

Eli leaned toward me bringing us face to face. "No, I know I'm funny; there's a difference."

I could feel his breath on my cheeks. "It's called arrogance," I alleged trying not to sound as disturbed as I was by his closeness.

I brought my eyes up from inspecting my hands to meet his eyes and my breath caught; I was momentarily stunned stupid. We were close enough to kiss. His eyes were like liquid silver; my heart beat erratically in my chest.

I took a step back. "Uh, you know, about earlier." I tried to sound as if our closeness hadn't affected me. I cleared my throat as I took another tiny step back and immediately felt the warmth of his body evaporate in the breeze.

"I know what you did in there wasn't real, so I won't hold you to that date. But thanks for helping shut her up. I've had a pretty rough week already." There that sounded intelligent and not at all childish, right?

An unfamiliar expression crossed his face, and he frowned as if I'd just slapped him. He moved out of my path, clearly taken back by my words; and I could have sworn as I was walking away, he whispered, "I wasn't playing, Grace." But then again, I had to be hearing things, because he was my best friend's brother; and, yeah, I'd had a crush on him practically since we met. That didn't mean he felt the same.

I made it through the rest of the day, not in a hurry to go home. I was dreading the conversation I was going to have to have with my mom once I got there. But, as usual, inevitability won, and the school day ended.

Evie was tutoring again today, and Eli was nowhere to be seen; but with the awkwardness that ensued earlier, I wasn't really feeling like dealing with him either.

So, I took a brooding walk home, stewing in the emotions from the last few days: Eli acting weird; Evie being all M.I.A.; Mom's near panic attack this morning; my weird dreams; the broken butterfly that was suddenly perfect; the tingling ache between my shoulders that was rapidly turning into borderline unbearable pain; Abby's renewed since of duty to keep me in geek check; and my seventeenth birthday only a couple of weeks away, with no real contact with any family other than my mom.

I wanted to lock myself in my bedroom and have a good full-faced ugly cry. And I'm not much of a crier.

All too soon I was home. I gripped the doorknob and strengthened myself for the lecture that was bound to come.

In a million years, I could never have prepared myself for what awaited me on the other side of the door.

CHAPTER SEVEN

I walked in the front door, prepared to go head-to-head with my mom, when I was assaulted with the brightest light I'd ever seen. I couldn't see where I was going so, I called out to her, "Hey, I'm home!" All I could think was where is this bright light coming from? "Ugg, I can't see, can you turn off whatever it is that's shining like the sun... Mom... Mom?"

I could hear a muffled conversation coming from the kitchen area, so I tried to feel my way there. I bumped into the entry table; something crashed and broke on the floor.

I managed to feel my way to the dining area relatively easily with only knocking over a few more minor things, not counting whatever the loudest crash was. Whatever the light was, I could tell it was getting brighter.

I caught a few snatches of conversation, an argument?

"It's forbidden; she cannot know. I'm sorry, Anna, I wish there was something I could do about it. Really, I do, but this is the way it must be," a deep, rough-edged manly voice tersely said.

"No, Raguel, this is not happening; she will not go through what I had to endure, what our ancestors endured. No!"

He seemed to soften at her adamancy; I could hear shuffling and moving.

"Anna, you know this is the way it is. She's been called for awakening. Whether you want it to happen or not, it is happening, and shouldn't she have the best tools available for the job?"

"I'm sorry, you're right; it's just too much for a little girl," she relented with a sniffle.

"Mom, are you in here?" I called, though I knew she was.

"Yes, honey, I am. You can come in now," she claimed as she composed her voice.

"Mom, I can't see, and I think I broke something a few minutes ago. Hey, where is that light coming from? Did you decide to ask the sun to visit?" I giggled at my own joke

"Oh, excuse me. I'm sorry that's my fault. Please don't be afraid, Grace." That same masculine voice boomed.

It seemed as if he put himself on a dimmer switch and turned the brightness down to the wattage of an ordinary night light with this eerie golden glow about it.

Yeah, that's right the man, being, thing, turned his "light" down.

If he stood, he'd be at least eight feet tall. He was shaped like a man, or rather the outline of a man, that was dipped in a blaze so bright he had no features.

I suppose that maybe he had features, but I just couldn't comprehend them. A being, that was made of light, that's what he was, and he was here sitting at my kitchen table talking to my mother as if they were old friends.

He seemed to study me, as I studied him. I swear my jaw hit the floor. I couldn't quit gawking, but it was like staring directly into an eclipse. It made my eyes water, and when I did blink or look away, his shape was still there, outlined and permanently etched in my brain.

My mother got up, walked over to me, and placed her hands on both of my shoulders hugging me to her.

"Grace, have a seat. This is Raguel. He's here to help you." She guided me to the closest chair.

Apparently, I lost all coherent brain functions, because I couldn't form words, nor could I remember how to walk. Did my mom board a crazy train to Mars when I went to school today? Seriously, what on earth was this thing that's here to help me?

"So, you might be wondering who Raguel is," my mother began.

"Are you serious, who he is isn't the first question that pops into my mind." Yep she boarded the crazy train.

Raguel snickered, clearly finding this humorous. He cleared his throat, and I turned to continue studying him.

In the time it took me to look from him to my mother and back to him again, he'd changed into a real man.

He still was tall, at least six and a half feet, body-builder-type muscles, and had dark dirty blonde hair shaved close to his scalp. He had the most amazing green eyes, like my mother's and mine. They looked like glowing crushed emeralds were embedded in them, where ours were more that of fresh cut grass on a warm summer day. A dark five o'clock shadow blossomed over his square masculine jaw.

He looked every bit a warrior and very manly. Someone straight from military tour of duty or even a WWE wrestler. Serious business. "Maybe I can help with that," he asserted.

"Well, first of all, it would have been a lot easier if you hadn't started out looking like that... that... thing." I gestured wildly at where he was standing moments before. "Seriously, you were a burning supernova not fifteen seconds ago; now you look like a bad mama-jam-a. What gives? It's impossible."

"Grace, watch your tone, young lady." Leave it to Mom to be all parental when others were there to see.

"Sorry, I mean no disrespect, I'm just..." My mouth floundered like a dying fish on land.

"Yes, I know, seeing one of us for the first time can be quite a shock. It's all right." He leaned back in his chair and scrubbed his hand across his jaw then crossed his arms. I don't think he really knew how to address the situation at hand either.

"My name is Raguel. I am an archangel in God's United Evangelical Secret Service, GUESS, as it's better known. In simplified terms, that means I train young humans and other warriors who have been called upon by God to serve him in the war that has been brewing between heaven and hell since the dawn of creation."

I blinked, blankly. Mom sniffled and pulled a Kleenex from the box on the table. I had never seen my mom cry so much in my life. Raguel continued his explanation without missing a beat. His voice suddenly went all official.

"Grace Noel Givings, you have been called upon for duty and marked as one of his own. You are bound by your blood. You are the daughter of a martyr and a child of a prince of heaven. You, by your own rights, are a princess of heaven. It is prophesied that you will become a great warrior and will ultimately bring peace between heaven and the agents of hell."

At one time, several things clicked into place: this man was certifiably crazy, I absolutely had lost my mind, and my mother was an emotional train wreck. I laughed hysterically.

I was laughing so hard I started crying and snorting and convulsing in my chair. Raguel looked exasperated, and my mother just stared at me unsure of what to do to calm me down, as if I had possibly sprouted a second head. Who knew, with the way this conversation started and twisted, maybe I had.

Raguel moved, knelt before me, and held a small black rectangular box out in front of him, placing his hands in mine. A jolt of energy seemed to pass between us. Unlike when it happened earlier with Eli, Raguel seemed to balance the charge.

I looked from the box in my hands with the tiny pink ribbon wrapped around it, back up to the man kneeling before me. He was being serious. The idiotic smile was wiped from my face by the intensity in his gaze.

"Grace, do you understand what I have just told you?"

"Yes... no... I... I don't know," I whispered, shaking my head in disbelief.

He smiled flashing brilliant straight white teeth. "That's okay, you will in time. When you are ready, open the box, but you do not have very long. Your training will begin in the morning. I'm sorry you don't have more time to come to terms with all of this, but it's rather extenuating circumstances and very imperative we start training right away. Your mother knows the way to the training center."

He stood, patted my hands, kissed the top of my downcast head, walked over to my mother, and embraced her as she sat.

"She is so much like you, Anna. So full of life, it's refreshing." He seemed almost proud of that fact. A stranger, no, a strange being was proud I was like my mother.

He cast another glance in my direction and began to glow again, brighter and brighter until the light burst, and tiny particles glittered in the room before they evaporated into thin air with an audible pop.

My mother cleared her throat and placed a fragile hand over mine. "I'm so sorry, Grace." She cracked. "I had hoped that this wouldn't happen to you." She sniffled and pulled another tissue from the box.

"How did you know about the dreams?" I asked still not piecing any of the larger puzzle together.

"My father was a preacher. He would have dreams and visions. Some were of the past, some of the future." She breathed out staring into space. "He began to preach his sermons over what he would see, drawing in large crowds of people." She swallowed and closed her eyes. Tears silently streamed down her face.

"When I was a young girl around eight, my brother Daniel was born." She wiped her cheeks and continued. "My father grew increasingly paranoid. He'd often lock my brother away and insist that he couldn't leave the house." She blew her nose and tucked a lock of hair behind her ear.

"When Danny was twelve, we were sitting in church listening to daddy preach." Her tears flowed more freely now. "Men burst into the room and executed my father in front of the entire congregation. They then proceeded to interrogate the rest of us, looking for those who belonged to his bloodline. It was a threat to the almighty Lucifer." She looked up and into my eyes.

"My mother told me to run and hide, and she'd send Danny to me. Protect your brother at all cost she whispered." She looked at the table once again still far away in her memory.

"Danny never made it to me, he and my mother were both captured and executed to prevent the bloodline from growing. They didn't know about me; if they did, they didn't care because I was a girl." She wiped away her tears again.

"That's where the angel found me. I was hiding in a secret box just barely large enough for two, under the pulpit. He whisked me away and told me that I was the single carrier left of the bloodline and that I needed to keep moving and keep it protected." She swallowed.

"I never stopped moving and he never stopped protecting me. It wasn't long before we fell in love, and not long after that, we found out that we were expecting a child." She looked at our clasped hands.

"You were the light of our lives. We knew you were special. He made me promise to keep moving, to protect you." She sniffled.

"Then why did we stop here? Why in this small Texas town?" I wondered out loud.

She shrugged her shoulders. "When you were six, your father came to me in a dream. He told me we were safe that we could stay here. Lucifer was no longer hunting our bloodline."

My mother sniffled as she turned to me and removed the tiny package from my hands. "Do you want to talk about any of this?" she asked.

I couldn't bring myself to form words, so I shook my head instead, grabbed the package off the table where she had set it, and raced upstairs to slam my door and cry, Lucky trailed my heels. I couldn't deal with my mother right now.

My phone buzzed, probably Evie. I couldn't deal with her right now, either.

I threw myself on my bed and preceded to bury my face in the blanket, just before the first tear finished falling down my cheek.

I didn't usually cry, but when I did, it was messy. Snot ran down my face; I got red, swollen eyes; my ordinarily small, upturned nose enlarged to swallow half my face; and my lips swelled like a bee had stung them. And we won't even start with the noises I made. I was pretty sure the term ugly cry was created just for me.

Lucky curled himself into a tiny ball right up against my chest, his warmth comforting me as I wailed. The package was lost amongst the tangle of pillows and blankets and bodies on the bed.

I cried for everything, everything I had lost, everything I had gained, everything I didn't understand. I cried for hours, until

I cried myself out and fell asleep listening to the loud snores of the warm, fuzzy little body next to me.

I remembered the fading thought as I fell asleep. What I wouldn't give to trade places with Lucky; he truly was like his namesake.

CHAPTER EIGHT

"Hello, child," a warm and assuring voice drawled.

I was in a vast and empty room with walls of the purest white; it was every color and no color at the same time. The floor held rolling fields of clouds, ever moving, ever changing, but still the same. Light poured from everywhere and nowhere at once. I searched for the owner of the voice but couldn't see him.

"Hello, child." his cheery voice repeated. I turned circles until I found him. He looked the same as the last time I had seen him—molten silvered hair, long flowing white tunic, moony eyes, ancient and yet somehow impossibly young. He was breathtaking.

"You have come seeking answers, have you not?" he asked, as his head tilted to the side and his hands gestured for me to come forward.

"I... I don't know," I stammered, answering honestly.

He chuckled. "Still trying to figure out the world around you?" He clicked his tongue, as one would chastise an ornery child. "It's best to focus on conquering one problem at a time dear."

He turned, taking my hand and linking our arms. "Come, take a walk with me." I'm pretty sure I didn't have a choice.

"How shall I start this epic tale?" he asked, lost in thought.

As we walked, the landscape began changing. A beautiful garden sprouted before me with ripening fruits, and berries on bushes, vines clinging to trees; and the greenest grass I'd ever seen sprung up beneath my feet. Flowers I'd never seen before were blooming in front of my eyes, permeating the air with their exotic perfumes.

"A long time ago, I created the earth. I created man, and woman, humans, to be my children on the earth. But before that, I created heaven, and my children there. I created them all unique and special." As he talked, I saw the scene play out before my eyes.

"Almost immediately, my children in heaven became jealous of my children on earth. They despised my growing fondness of the new species. They began fearing that humans would soon replace them in my favor, so the angels created an army to overthrow the human influence."

He paused while I watched Lucifer persuade the rebellious angels into his army. I watched the ensuing argument and banishment. Though I'd been taught my whole life about this, it was amazing and new to watch it unfold before my very eyes.

"I banished Lucifer and his rebellious army from heaven. They fell like stars scattered throughout the cosmos. Most were banished to the lake of fire. I placed rules for all the remaining angels and humans to follow. First, the humans were not to eat of the fruit of knowledge. Second, Lucifer would be chained for 1,000 years and loosed only once a season, once a lifetime. Third, I forbade my angels from pursuing relationships with humans"

I watched Lucifer being chained through the bars on the gates of hell. It was painful and agonizing to see.

"After the first attempt to overthrow me, I thought he'd learned his lesson," he paused and shook his head sadly, "but he tempted Eve with the forbidden fruit, and subsequently created sin. I knew then that he was never going to change and made ready a failsafe, so to speak."

He paused and handed me a gold-encrusted hand mirror, he procured out of thin air. It was antique and beautiful.

"Once in a millennium, a great and powerful warrior is born. Some are called upon to keep Lucifer from creating the end of days, when he is released, and to re-chain him when the time comes. Lucifer is striving to end the human existence; he blames all of them for his abandonment in hell. He takes no responsibility for his actions. His vanity and pride are extensive." He stopped and faced me and shook his head as if to erase the thoughts there.

"These warriors are all from the same bloodline; they are martyrs for my cause. This, Grace, is your mother's bloodline, your ancestors. On the day you turned thirteen, Lucifer was released from his imprisonment and began his seven-year reign over the earth." He gave me a sadden look.

"Three years have passed with Lucifer in command. He has put himself in a place of power to control the worlds money, food, military and laws." He patted my hand

"Once a warrior is called for awakening, his blood will become aware of the past conflicts; it is blood memory of sorts. You relive lives of your ancestors until you gain the knowledge needed from the previous lives," he continued as if to answer my unspoken question.

"So, my dreams, they really aren't dreams?" I asked bewildered

"No, they are not. You are the first female to possess the Hashem, the consuming fire. Along with that, there is an ancient prophesy that states, when the prophet and the law giver are publicly killed, the end of days begins." He paused a moment to let his words sink in before he continued.

"It has come to my attention that the descendants of Moses, the law giver, and Elijah, the prophet, are amongst the earth once again. Lucifer is desperately trying to find them." He pleaded with me. "You must find them first. You must save them. Your ancestors have left tools amongst the earth; you will need these items. That is one of them." He gestured to the looking glass in my hands.

"Why me? I'm just a kid. I can barely walk on two feet, much less save two people and prevent a war, and ultimately Armageddon," I pleaded, needing him to understand that I was one human girl.

He just stared at me hopefully as my thoughts turned ever grimmer.

"Is my destiny to watch helpless as the end of earth comes and Lucifer reigns free, because I'm too weak, too young, and too pathetic to protect the world?" I didn't understand why I was chosen for this.

"No, Grace, there is no such thing as destiny. That is a human word. You must first understand. You are unique. I made you in my image like no other. I divined in you great gifts." He placed his hands on my shoulders. "You, Grace, are like no warrior who has come before you; you are a child of heaven and earth."

"You know, that is the second time I've heard that today, and I don't understand it any more than I did the first time!" I sighed, becoming frustrated for the lack of understanding.

"Wait, my mother told me she fell in love with an angel and had me. Who is my father? Can I meet him?" I looked around trying to see if he was here with us.

"No, I cannot, and will not give you the answers you seek, there. Not yet. In due time. Remember, Grace, it was forbidden that angels and humans fall in love. Your father and mother broke the rules; he is being punished, and your mother was forbidden to speak about him."

"I don't understand. What are you saying? That I was a mistake, that I should never have been? If this is the case, then how would I be able to put a stop to Lucifer once and for all?"

I was beginning to grow angry. I could feel the heat reddening my cheeks. I wanted nothing more out of life than to find the rest of my family, the links that connected me with this world, any world, and yet here was the one being that could give me the answers and he refused.

"You sound a lot like Job." He looked greatly saddened; I would have sworn tears were forming in his eyes. "I am not being cruel, Grace. I understand your heart better than any other."

He shook his head chasing yet another thought. "You miss the point. I created humanity with free will, but it has been corrupted and warped. You have a pure light that you need to shine for all the human world to see. You are everything I hoped humanity would be, the best of both worlds. I see goodness and love, hope and humility in you, Grace. You are stronger than you believe you are. You are bestowed with many gifts you have yet to acknowledge. You will vanquish those who threaten your light; you were born the purest heart." He pulled me to him and hugged me protectively.

"You will make great and powerful enemies this day. You must never doubt your own strength. But I have faith in you," he all but whispered. With one last squeeze, he let me go. I could see his silhouette fade from the bright room.

I blinked back a few stray tears of my own and awoke. I once again was lying curled up with Lucky in a heap on my bed, and the beautiful antique looking glass curled in my fingers. My body ached from exhaustion, and my back still burned and tingled.

The clock on my desk read 5:00 a.m. No way was I going to go back to sleep after that. I got up and found a note from my mom, right next to the little black box with the pink bow.

Grace,

Today starts your training; we need to leave by 6:00 a.m.

Love, Mom

I had no idea what training would consist of, so I threw some school clothes in a bag, shoved the little black box with the bow in the bag, along with the newly procured mirror, put on a t-shirt, sweat pants and tennis shoes, and threw my hair in a knot on my head, then called it good and left the room in a hurry.

"Let's do this! Shall we?" I muttered to Lucky as he trailed me out of the room.

CHAPTER NINE

Mom pulled up to an old run-down building, that most assuredly had long ago seen better days, in the middle of the absolute worst part of town imaginable. A dilapidated Dollar Store sat to the right; most of its neon sign was missing letters except for the d, o, and r.

To the left sat a hole-in-the-wall gas station that had exactly two pumps. It was the kind of gas station that had more sales from sodas, candy bars, alcohol, and cigarettes than it did from gas. The store clerk sat on the raised edge of the pumps practicing blowing out smoke rings from her lighted cigarette.

Her white-washed bobbed hair was mussed, and her worker's vest hung off her slumped shoulders as if it were four sizes too big. Talk about classy. I would have been afraid to be outside alone given the neighborhood and surroundings.

The building I was supposed to venture into had no lights on. The windows were boarded up with the words "No Trespassing" painted across the plywood sheets. The flaking, white painted walls were littered with graffiti, using every curse word under the sun, plus a few I didn't know.

Vulgar images were spray-painted over them, making blobs out of whatever body part it was. Stray cigarette butts were discarded everywhere, along with lots of trash from anything and everything.

"Really?" I squeaked. "This is the infamous training facility for GUESS? Couldn't God find a better place, a safer place, to train his so-called warriors?"

Mom shifted in her seat and gave me a small knowing smile. "You aren't using your eyes, Grace. You need to concentrate, strip away what your brain is telling you, and listen to what your heart is showing you."

"I am using my eyes. I have been for the last seventeen years, and I believe my eyesight is fine. Thank. You. Very. Much." I was growing more irritated and anxious by the second.

"Never mind, it's okay." She paused, and I could tell she wanted to say more. She shook her head as if to ward off her own thoughts. "I'll be here when it's time for school to be over." She leaned across the armrest and kissed my cheek.

I got out of the car and grabbed my bags; I hesitated when I got to the front door of the building, and I turned to see my mom as she waved from the driver's seat and pulled out an old, beat-up copy of some long-ago forgotten novel.

Feeling now completely abandoned and exposed in the destitute outdoors, I opened the door seeking what little shelter awaited inside.

I was immediately blown away. Raguel was in front of a full mirrored wall. He was quite the sight in a pair of grey sweat pants and a black tank top, and bare feet—I'd learn later that this attire was the mandatory training wear.

In his hands, he held a six-foot-long stick, or staff, essentially a wooden pole, with the middle wrapped in what appeared to be some type of black leather cord. I watched in awe as he leaped, jumped, danced, and twirled it about. Occasionally, he'd strike out at an invisible opponent. It was elegant and truly beautiful to watch.

At some point during his elaborate dance, he saw me standing there like a welcome mat, enamored with his handling of the stick.

"Come in, Grace. You can set your bags and shoes against the wall."

I did as I was told without uttering a single smart-mouthed retort. It was a miracle, though, because there were plenty on the tip of my tongue.

He gazed at me in the mirror, and I kind of felt a little violated when he was finished.

"Tomorrow, please wear tighter clothing; you're going to need to see how your body moves. Seeing how today is an introduction, so to speak, what you're wearing will suffice."

"Oh well, thanks, I suppose." Leaning up and stretching my arms above my head, I gestured to him and asked, "Am I going to learn that?"

"You may learn any and all of this," he gestured, waving a hand to encompass the whole room. To my surprise, there was almost every weapon imaginable stocked in the room, a real dream for a weapon fan, though I was a girl that didn't know weapons and couldn't name enough to count on both hands. It was still impressive to me, however.

As I looked around the room, I realized I honestly hadn't seen it for what it was. There were weight machines, combat dummies, and a sign pointing to a target range.

Upstairs was a walking track, a sign for the pool, and sauna leading downstairs. Bedrooms were on the fifth and sixth floors. I hadn't even realized the building had a second floor, much less a sixth.

"I think it's best that you learn to use your body first, though, because not always will you have a weapon available to use," he inclined his head in my direction interrupting my gawk fest.

My head whipped around quickly at his words. "You mean I'm going to learn to punch people?" I wasn't prepared for that; my mother had taught me not to hit, kick, or bite when I was still a little child.

"Yes, Grace. What did you expect? If we were able to peacefully talk, we would already have done so by now, and there wouldn't be a war." Okay, now he was just being facetious.

"Sorry, it's just; I've never done anything like this before. It pretty much goes against everything I've been taught. So, forgive me if I find it hard to do. Um, look at me." I gestured to my small frame. "I couldn't even intimidate a snail, much less demons!" I let out a sigh. "Besides, even if I did somehow manage to learn all of this, it would take years." I was already feeling slightly overwhelmed and defeated, and we'd not even started training yet.

"I know, I suppose she thought she was helping you." He seemed to pause and search for the right words to say. "Grace, you have more power in your one pinky than any other being on this planet. Aside from me, that is," he smirked and shrugged. "You need to embrace your future and believe in yourself."

 "This is a place of higher power," Raguel continued. "When you are here, time slows to a crawl. What may seem like hours to you are merely nano-seconds in the human world. You could, and likely will, spend entire weeks here, and only hours will have passed at home; a month may only be a weekend." He paused and looked up as the bell above the front door rang signaling its opening. "Ah, just in time. Here is your sparring partner now."

I turned to look but the sun had come up and was blinding against the dark blot. "Hey, sorry I'm running late!" said the blot.

That voice, I knew that voice. No way it was him. What is he doing here?

Lucas laughed and placed a tanned finger under my chin. "You might want to close that before bugs fly in. We do tend to have a few of those around here."

I blinked a few times and shook my head. While my brain scrambled to make sense of everything, I was learning and seeing; my synapsis fired but didn't register. "Wow." Smooth, Grace, open your mouth and say something intelligent why don't you? I thought. "Wow, uh… what are you doing here?" I finally stuttered out.

"We've been waiting for you to awaken a long time, Grace. Stories have been told about you around here for generations, and I'm lucky enough to be your friend and training partner." He wagged his eyebrows at my disbelief.

"I am the head student here at GUESS, so I suppose you could say rank has privileges." He shrugged.

"With Lucas here, it will help me watch your actions and maneuvers. That and you two will be fighting alongside one another when that time does come." Raguel clapped his large hands together. "Let's get started."

They then proceeded in kicking my rear end for the next hour and a half. When they finished, Lucas helped me stand. And Raguel would barely speak to me. He muttered something about an "infuriating little nit" as he walked to the showers.

I felt like I had spent more time on my butt than I had on my feet today. My back was even achier between my shoulder blades, but my whole body protested moving in general. I showered and dressed in a hurry.

I looked in the wall-length mirror and braced myself for the inevitable. I needed to see what this was on my back. It had gone on too long already.

I wiped the fog from the mirror and turned my back to face it. I closed my eyes, nerves getting the better of me. I readied myself and turned.

On my back, between my shoulder blades, was a glowing tattoo. It pulsed and radiated light, much as Raguel's whole body could do. The mark was shaped like two diamonds side by side, touching to form a weirdly beautiful infinity symbol. My heart stopped beating as I gasped.

I rushed to get dressed for school, trying my best to forget about the strange mark. As I walked out of the showers, Lucas walked up to me with a steaming to-go cup of something smelly. I scrunched up my face as a sort of protest, but he just laughed it off and forced the cup into my hands.

"It might stink, and it might taste worse than it smells, but, trust me, your body will thank you later."

I turned to leave, and then paused. "Thanks," I said gesturing to the cup. "So, um, see you at school?"

Lucas seemed focused on my back like he could see the mark. He looked as if he were about to reach out and touch it. "You bet," he replied on auto pilot before seeming to shake out of whatever trance he was in. "Oh, uh, Grace, obviously you can't tell anyone about me, not even Oliver, Evie or Eli."

"Yeah, I kind of figured." I tried to keep the duh out of my voice. I waved and headed out the door.

I faced a new reality as I walked through the doors, and outside to my mother's awaiting car.

A huge rounded front cathedral, complete with a wide and rounded sweeping staircase, stained glass windows and white marble columns, stood in place of the dilapidated building I had entered earlier this morning. I mean minutes ago. Boy that would take some getting used to.

Oh, sure, the rundown buildings still sat to either side, but the cathedral itself was in pristine condition. Security cameras blinked on and off at each corner of the building.

I stood in awe for a moment staring at the beautiful building before climbing into the car. I didn't take my eyes off of it until we turned the block and the building was out of sight.

CHAPTER TEN

By Friday at school, my body looked like it had one huge bruise covering it. I had been getting my butt kicked for hours twice daily for the last three days. I wasn't getting better; Lucas was trying to be supportive, but Raguel was only growing more agitated with me. At one point this morning, he even threw up his hands and shouted, "That's it; we're all doomed! I give up! You're not even trying anymore!" As he stormed off.

I'm not sure why he was so frustrated. I really was trying, and it wasn't like he was getting his tail end kicked from here to next Sunday on the daily. I looked to Lucas and squeaked,

"I am trying; I really am." Lucas, ever so patiently replied, "I know; just let him cool down. He's a bit of a hot head; actually, all arches are. Anyway, your body has taken a beating. You must be sore by now, and you aren't even complaining about it. Let's call it a day." He handed me another steaming cup of stench.

Everything did hurt, most especially, my back. I was beginning to become concerned. Maybe I needed to see a doctor, not that a doctor could understand what was on my back either. I showered my morning sweat off, and, as usual, rushed to get ready for school and pretend nothing was different about me.

I managed to scramble to school with a few minutes to spare. I dropped my backpack where I stood just outside my locker and tried to stretch my aching muscles.

While I was busy stretching out my aching back and replaying what happened with Raguel this morning, Eli walked up, essentially scaring the life out of me. I let out a yelp which only earned me one of his trademark laughs.

"Hey, short stuff; pick you up at seven tonight?"

I gave him a quizzical look and stared at him dumbfounded. "What are you talking about?"

He placed both hands on his heart and pretended to stumble about as if I'd stabbed him. "Oh you wound me!"

I kept giving him a you're-insane look as he wobbled around the hallway.

Finally, he gave up the charade. "Our date. Tonight, is Friday night. Dinner, dancing, moonlight, romance, remember?" He wagged his eyebrows.

"Right." I was still unsure of what he was getting at. "Have you thought about trying out for the school play? I heard they were casting Romeo." I laughed teasing him.

He smirked and leaned in closely to whisper, "Only if you'll be my Juliet". Was Abby around or something? I looked around. Nope, not here.

"Walk you to class?" he asked as he slung an arm over my backpack. My back gave a burning protest, and I winced a little with the added weight.

"Sure. Hey, where is Evie? I haven't seen her in days. I miss her."

"Oh, she's around. She's really mad at you, though; says she's texted you several times and you haven't texted her back." He chuckled

I winced again, this time not from the pain in my back. Man, I forgot. How can someone forget her own best friend?

"Oh no! I completely forgot to text her back. I've been doing a lot of after-school stuff, and by the time I get home I'm so tired I pass right out. I have to go find her and explain." I shrugged Eli's arm off and waved as I bounded off toward Evie.

"See you tonight. Oh and, Grace... wear something nice." He winked, oblivious to my inner struggle.

I groaned. Just what I needed, a fake date with the hottest boy in school, and my body looked like one giant black eye. One good thought was that purple really was my color.

I found Evie as her dark curly head bobbed into her first-period class.

"Evie," I shouted.

She turned to look and glared. Oh, boy. I was really in trouble.

I sprinted to catch up with her. "Evie, I'm so sorry; I can explain."

"You know, Grace, you aren't the only one who's busy, but if you called or texted me, I would have called or texted you back. Especially after three days. Three whole days." Her bottom lip trembled as tears threatened to spill out of her eyes.

I recoiled as her voice bounced and echoed down the hallway. I'm sure that would attract nosey people's attention.

"I'm really sorry. I've been having after-school activities and by the time I get home, I pass right out. It's no excuse, I know; I'm sorry, really, truly sorry. I'm a horrible friend."

That earned a sniffle and a small smirk. "Yes, you are a horrible friend. But you're the best horrible friend on the planet."

I smiled and hugged her. "Your brother and I have a date tonight and I'm at a fashion loss. I need the expert advice of the coolest girl in school. Know anyone available this afternoon to help? We can talk about what's bugging you then."

She gave a halfhearted shrug and a lopsided grin. "Of course, see you after school; I'll walk you home." With a quick flourishing wave, she disappeared behind the closing door of her first-period class.

I walked in to my classroom and took my seat. Mr. Withers was at it again, with one of his autopilot speeches about how we all pretty much are failures and "put forth minimal efforts in our homework". When he got on one of those rants, it usually lasted the entire period. This one was no exception.

I managed to make it to lunch without thinking about saving the world, my aching body, and the piercing pain in my back, only to find a pain in my butt—Eli waiting by my classroom door for me.

"Uh, hi." I looked at him quizzically unsure of what was happening.

"Hey, I thought I'd walk you to lunch. Is that okay?" he asked almost hesitantly.

"As if I could tell you no." I joked.

Eli shook his head and sighed. "Yeah, about that Grace, we really should talk. I've been meaning to talk to you about a few things for a while now actually. I…"

"Hey, Grace, Hey Eli!" Oliver walked up obliviously interrupting whatever was bothering Eli.

"Hey," we replied in unison.

"You guys coming or what?"

I turned to Eli with a question on my face.

"Uh, yeah, Ollie, be right there." He turned to me an unreadable look flashed in his eyes. "We can talk about it later." He patted my crossed arms.

"Are you sure?"

"Yeah, after all, we do have a date tonight." He smirked and turned to catch up with Oliver.

My back began to throb to the rhythm of my heartbeat. I blinked to fight back the tears, but my efforts were futile, as the pain came barreling back.

Time slowed to a crawl as I clung to a nearby desk. Eli kept looking over his shoulder at me as he and Oliver advanced down the hall, and, I swear, I could see storm clouds gathering in his eyes.

The lights in the hall strobed in time to the throbbing in my back. With each beat of my heart and each glance from Eli my mark would pulse, growing more intense with each passing breath. And it seemed as if the wind picked up in the hall out of nowhere, and papers floated in the air drawn toward Eli as he passed.

As quickly as it started, it all stopped. In the next blink everything was fine. Nothing littered the ground, and the wind died. Had I been hallucinating due to pain?

Eli turned and stopped and made an "are you okay" face. I waved him off as I wiped the tears from my cheeks. It wasn't as if I could explain to him what I just witnessed. I wasn't even sure what I'd seen. Right then I made a promise to myself to find out why the mark was causing my back to hurt.

School seemed to speed by; classes blurred into more classes until it was over. Evie met me in the hall flashing borrowed car keys. "I believe we have some shopping to do."

Shopping was one of Evie's favorite pastimes. She always managed a polished, yet effortless, look, where I opted more for the relaxed slacker look.

We'd made it to the mall in record-breaking time. She found several tops that screamed her name, while I settled on a sheer, pastel-pink, floral printed peplum top with eyelet lace trim and pearl buttons.

"That is adorable; Eli is going to love it on you. Hey, I even have the perfect heels that match. Oh, you're going to look ravishing!" she gushed.

"Yay!" I mocked with fake enthusiasm. Evie rolled her eyes as we made our way to the checkout counter.

I forked over the pizza money from the other night, hesitant that maybe I should have saved it to pay for my portion of dinner. Being a tutor didn't pay that much money.

My nerves were getting the better of me. I was nearly silent on the ride home. Stress and lack of sleep were catching up to me quickly.

Evie prattled on about who knows what, while I stewed in my own self-pity. I guess I should have just been she'd started talking to me again. But sometimes when the girl got started, she didn't know when to stop.

After a quick detour by Evie's for the shoes, we finally made it to my house. I realized that it was nearing six o'clock and I only had an hour to get ready for my first date. Real or otherwise, it would still be my first ever. Evie trailed me up the stairs, continuing her rant.

"Earth to Grace. How are you going to wear your hair? And please tell me you are going to put on makeup?"

"Do I look that bad?" I tried for mock horror, but I think it came out more like real horror.

The truth was I had very dark circles under my eyes and purple and green bruises forming all up and down my arms. I was a mess, and nothing short of a miracle would make it better.

"Help!" I squeaked as I shimmied into my dark-wash skinny jeans.

"Evie to the rescue." She mocked in superhero fashion.

Half an hour later, I was ready, makeup applied, and hair curled. Mom knocked on the door.

"I believe there is a very nervous young man in the living room asking for you."

I turned to Evie wide-eyed. "Am I ready?" I asked.

"Do you doubt me?" she replied in a huff.

My mother gasped at the sight of me. "Grace, you look lovely!" She kissed me on the cheek. "Have fun tonight, sweetheart."

"I will; thanks, Mom!"

"What? No thanks for me?" Evie exclaimed.

"Of course, thank you for rescuing me in my time of desperate fashion need." This whole ordeal had made me nervous and unsure of myself.

"That's more like it," she replied. "Now get down there before he thinks you've changed your mind." I readied myself and walked out of the bedroom.

CHAPTER ELEVEN

I descended the stairs in record time, trying my best not to trip over my own two feet on the way down. At the bottom of the stairs, stood a very handsome young man, indeed.

He wore a solid button up blue shirt that made his steel grey eyes seem bluer than silver. His hair was expertly styled, and he was nervously pacing the floor.

I let out a little giggle. "You better watch it, or you'll wear a path in my mom's carpet."

He looked up at me and his eyes lit up with fire. I had read many books about boys looking at girls with heated looks; I had even seen it on TV and in the movies. But to have all that unabated attention focused on you was enough to make any girl swoon, especially when it was a boy you always dreamed would like you. It just didn't seem real. It made me nervous and my heart all fluttery.

I cleared my throat to try and steady myself. I looked at my shoes, uncomfortable with the look in his eyes and silence in the room. "Do I look okay? I mean, you never really said where we were going so, I wasn't sure what I should wear. If I need to change, I can." I rambled as I made a move like I was headed back upstairs.

"No," he whispered. "No." he paused and was louder this time. "You look great, more than great; actually, you look perfect!"

I smiled, and he beamed. "Oh, here are your keys. Thanks for letting us borrow your car earlier." I held them out dangling between us.

"You're welcome to borrow it anytime; it was worth it."

He moved to open the door as I turned and called up the stairs, knowing that both Evie and my mother were eavesdropping. "Bye, don't wait up." You could hear their fast shuffling footsteps as they raced back to my bedroom.

"Bye," they called back in unison all nonchalantly. I laughed and shook my head as I turned to meet Eli at the door.

Eli was the perfect gentleman, as he opened the car door for me to climb in.

It took almost the whole thirty-minute ride to the restaurant for conversation to get started. It seemed awkward with this boy I'd known forever. He'd seen me at my worst and my best and everything in between. But somehow in this car alone with him now, it just seemed different.

I was fidgety with nerves in the silence. He kept stealing glances, when he thought I wasn't looking, as if I weren't there, or maybe any second, I would disappear. I knew how he felt. Was this real?

His car smelled like the worn leather seats and his cologne, forest meets ocean. I saw the streetlights dance across his face as we made the trek through the more populated city. His eyes glowing with anticipation.

I suppose I had picked at a frayed string on my shirt long enough that it made Eli laugh and lean over and take my hand in his. I looked up from our joined hands and met his steely gaze.

"It's okay. You don't have to be so nervous. I don't bite." He flashed a wicked grin. "Besides, it would be a pity to ruin such a nice shirt," he teased again, which made my heart speed up a notch more in response. It was entering heart attack speed.

"Oh, you really should go back to being quiet. You are much more attractive when you don't open your mouth." I huffed and crossed my arms in mock anger, a smile playing on my lips.

"I happen to know for a fact that you do bite." I raised an eyebrow at him as I continued to taunt. "Remember when we were five and you bit me because I was using your blue Crayon to draw a flower?"

His eyes rounded with remembered horror. "I have never seen my sister fly through the air to attack me like some sort of deranged spider monkey before. I learned my lesson that day. Grace is off limits." He laughed, showcasing his dreamy smile and dimpled cheeks.

I giggled and relaxed back into the seat a smile still plastered on my face. "There's my girl." He said as he rested his hand on the compact armrest, barely brushing mine. His girl. My mind screamed internally while all the butterflies that took residence in my stomach did summersaults and high-fived each other.

Somewhere along the road, the cloudy evening turned menacing. It had started to pour outside. Eli made circles in the parking lot, presumably to find a close parking spot, with no luck.

We parked at the edge of the lot around the far-right side of the building furthest from the door. At the rate the rain was falling in fat drops, we would be drenched before we reached the entrance.

We sat in silence for a while before Eli sighed.

"It's not looking like it's going to let up anytime soon. Let's make a break for it on three."

I nodded at his words and readied myself for the storm. On his mark, I raced around the front of the car where he was waiting, hand extended to help steady me. We raced for the safety of the awning in the front where a large crowd was gathered to wait out the rainstorm.

My shirt clung to me, and my pants were soaked almost to the knee. I could feel my hair limp and plastered to my face. I felt like a drowned rat. Eli looked no worse for wear, a little wet but still well put together. He never released my hand as he opened the door for me and gave the hostess his name.

It was fancy inside—intimate tables with white linens and wine glasses ready and waiting to be used, and candles flickering in the middle with each draft from the vents or movements from people passing by.

The hostess led us to a table in the far back; I suppose she knew we'd want privacy. The dining chairs were a plush burgundy and oak. Expensive wallpaper in burgundy and gold lined the walls, and matching carpet covered the floor.

I'd never been to a restaurant like this before. It was the kind of place that business men and women would take clients they wanted to impress on working lunches and dinners. I would never be able to afford this kind of fancy in my everyday life. It felt surreal.

After glancing over the menu, I decided on the grilled chicken salad, not because I was one of those girls, but because it was the cheapest thing on there. If I had to pay tonight, I wanted to make sure I could afford my own meal.

The waitress came, and we ordered. Neither one of us had spoken a word to each other since we'd been seated, each appearing to be preoccupied with the menu longer than necessary. Feeling a bit awkward, I excused myself to the restroom.

As I feared, my hair was plastered to my face and beginning to curl with the air drying it. My mascara had smudged under my eyes, and while my shirt was thin enough and already nearly dry, my pants were still soaked. I quickly grabbed some paper towels and wiped under my eyes to remove the smudges. I finger-combed my hair and tried to dry as much of my pants as I could using the hand dryers.

I stepped out of the bathroom looking slightly less horrible than when I had entered it. I had hoped that maybe I could salvage this haphazard date. But as I wove my way back to the table, I realized Eli wasn't alone. In fact, it appeared I wasn't welcome.

Abby McClure had replaced me in the seat across from Eli. Her pink lipstick was stained on his cheek; it felt like an audible slap in my face. He gazed across the table at her while she gibbered on about something on the menu.

I stood frozen in place feeling like a voyeur spying without interrupting. I could feel the moment their betrayal hit my soul, like a fist squeezing my heart.

I wanted to die right there. Is this why he'd asked me out? Is this why he'd brought me here? Eli must have felt my burning gaze, because in one fluid motion he shoved at the table scooting his chair back with a loud screech, as if Abby were lava that would burn him, ultimately breaking their intimate moment and sending both glasses of ice water into Abby's lap.

"You!" yelped Abby as ice shot down the front of her now nearly see-through blouse.

Eli shot her a dark look before he took a step toward me. He was flushed, and the anguish I saw in his face didn't match the bright princess-pink lipstick smeared across his cheek, or the ache where my heart had shattered in my chest.

I pulled in a deep breath and tried to calm myself, fighting the burning tears I hoped weren't visible. I wasn't going to give Eli and Abby the cruel satisfaction of seeing me cry. It was enough that she was even here sitting in my chair and all these innocent patrons had become front-row-seated participants to the spectacle that was my social life.

When I finally thought I had myself calm enough to face him, I met his eyes with my own. I was bluffing of course; I had let myself begin to believe he liked me, not her. In my heart I knew it was too good to be true. People like him didn't like or date people like me.

Salvaging as much pride and tiny fragments of my shattered heart as I could, I faked indifference to the situation.

"Oh, well, I see Abby could make it after all. If you'll both excuse me, I'm going to cancel my food order. I'll just be getting out of your way then." I waved to the waiter hiding inconspicuously behind the wall of ferns.

"Yeah, you better." Abby sneered. Wow, what an intelligent comeback. She had some nerve.

Eli took another tentative step toward me and tried to reach for my arm, but I jerked away from his grip before he could even touch me.

"Grace..." he gasped as if I'd punched him. In that moment, I could have. I really wanted to. I was angry and hurt and humiliated.

"No, Eli, you don't get to make excuses for this," I exclaimed, louder and with more hurt than I intended to show.

"Grace, please listen..." he pleaded begging me with his eyes not to leave.

"Just let her go," said Abby joyful at my humiliation.

"Shut up, Abby. Haven't you done enough?" Eli shouted. He turned to me, remorse pinching his face. Other restaurant patrons were beginning to complain, and more waitresses and waiters were hiding in plain sight just to hear and watch the spectacle we were making.

I shook my head no to silence him. Imploring him with my eyes just to let me go.

"Goodbye," I whispered as I turned on my heel and blew past tables of gawkers, bypassing trays of food and wait staff. I didn't want anyone else to see me hurting.

I didn't care about causing a scene anymore; I just had to escape this mess. I shoved outside as the first of what felt like would be many tears slid down my cheeks. I slipped around people waiting under the awning, and out into the night.

When the first icy rain drops splat in my face and the wind slapped my hair about, I only then remembered I was stranded. Eli had driven me here; Mom's car was at home.

"Great!" I muttered to myself, kicking an invisible rock, as I wiped at my eyes in an increasingly futile attempt to keep my mascara from smearing any further. I sat on the curb in the pouring rain and continued to contemplate my predicament. After all, nothing worse could happen to me tonight.

Taking stock of my situation I stood and began to pace again. I was so lost in my thoughts, that I wasn't paying any attention to where I was going. I just drifted the parking lot stunned.

I didn't want to ride home with the person who shredded my heart. I could call my mom but that would only add further insult to injury. I had less than twenty dollars to my name, wadded and shoved in my pocket. That wasn't enough for cab fare home.

I was too busy thinking about my predicament and counting the change in my pocket to watch where I was going. Without warning, time slowed and crawled.

Darkness enveloped me thick and misty as fog. My heartbeat pounded with the cadence of the rain splattering the nearby roof. I faltered in my steps wondering what had happened to the lights on this side of the building and ran right into a man masked so far in shadow he looked void of any and all light.

His eyes were like two starless and empty orbs in his face. He smelled strongly of fire and ash, but I couldn't make out any more of his murky features.

This corner of the building was soaked in the shadows and rain falling from the sky. A feeling of unease crept up my spine. I felt like a fly trapped in a web with the spider close by waiting to devour his prey.

"I'm so sorry." I shivered and squeaked ducking back out into the rain and lit parking area. I scurried as fast as I could to the nearest street lamp, feeling the eyes of that man following me. I walked out into the glow of the street lights following them around and back to the front of the building toward the safety of people.

The hair on the back of my neck continued to stand on end. With each beat of my heart, the void moved closer. Street lamps turned off one at a time as the darkness touched them following in my wake.

I could feel whatever it was getting closer. My breath went out in a puff of white fog. The temperature dropped rapidly. I began to shiver, fear and the cold clouding my thoughts.

My mark burned agonizingly against my back, as if some living thing were scratching and clawing from the inside trying to be released. I bent over breathless trying hard not to lose my balance. The excruciating pain almost had me blacking out.

When I had made it to the front of the restaurant, time thundered back in to place. My beating heart still pounded as I plopped myself down onto the curb again, exhaustion beckoning my weary heart. Lightning suddenly cracked above me fracturing the night sky. I found it odd because that was exactly what I felt like inside. Fractured.

I turned to look behind me, still cautious of my surroundings and still feeling a bit on edge. The man in the shadows wasn't there anymore. It was as if he had been swallowed whole by the darkness just outside the safety of the lighted circle my street lamp made on the concrete. Another lightning bolt crashed, and all the lights came back on.

I stood and turned to race back to the safety of the awning when I realized Eli was standing right behind me. I flinched, shocked that he was standing there. He had a strange look on his face, a combination of fury, remorse, sadness, and something else I couldn't decipher. Somewhere between here and there, he had lost Abby's lipstick on his cheek, and from the smells wafting out of the bag he was carrying, he had gotten our dinner to go.

It only ignited my anger, enraging me further. He had no right to be angry or hurt. In that moment I wish I'd have slapped him. He would have deserved it for everything he put me through. Honestly, he deserved a whole lot more than that. However, deserving or not, violence was not acceptable. I thought we were at least friends. I should have known better.

"May I please take you home?" he asked, though I could tell his heart wasn't in it. If I'd accept, it'd be a pity ride. Talk about pouring salt in a wound.

I shook my head. "No, that's okay. I was planning on calling my mom." I stepped up on to the curb, ready to walk away. I was trying hard to hold on to my dignity and failing to grasp the reign on my temper. I really wanted to ask why he was even out here, especially when Abby was inside waiting for him. But I didn't. I thought it'd be best left unspoken. I didn't need to be as petty as Abby.

He wiped his hand down his face in frustration, as if he could wipe away all the events from the last hour. He moved around me, opened the driver's side door of his car, and plopped the melting bag in the back seat. After slamming the door shut again, he walked back to me.

With him in the parking lot and me in heels on the sidewalk, we were eye level. He was close enough that I could feel his body heat radiating off him. I wanted to move, but I didn't want to give him the satisfaction of knowing his being this close to me made me uncomfortable.

I raised my eyes to meet his, determined not to show my intimidation. This close I could see his irises swirling like liquid silver. I could feel his heated breath exhale across my face. I was overwhelmed by him.

"Please, Grace, I won't ask anything from you again if you'll just let me take you home. It isn't safe out here, and it's raining, if you haven't noticed," he pleaded.

I backed away turning to leave, determined not to get back in the car with him. "There's plenty of light from the street lamps and it's not a far walk home. I can manage," I lied through my teeth.

I was terrified of whatever that thing was, whoever was watching me from the shadows, and it was a horribly long walk home, not counting the storm.

"Please." Was his only reply. He grabbed for my hand and pulled me back to him. "Enough lighted walking path for you to walk home, you say?" he huffed through clenched teeth.

He blinked and for the second time in mere minutes, time paused again. It was as if I could reach out and move the raindrops like a curtain, positioned in their decent by sheer force of will. I reached up and touched one and it burst on my finger.

Eli's silver eyes seemed to glow and swirled as if stirred by his emotions. Lightning crashed again striking a nearby power transformer. The entire block's electricity went out.

"Where are the lights now, Grace?" he asked angrily.

This close in proximity I couldn't speak. I really didn't want to be trapped in a car with the boy who just stomped my heart into millions of tiny pieces in front of the one person in the world I wouldn't want to have witnessed it.

I just shook my head no, not trusting my voice. But before I could refuse his offer again, he moved even closer, his large frame towering over me. My chest brushed his when I exhaled.

I watched through streaks of lightning as a drop of rain clung on to his bangs for dear life before finally giving in to its descent down his face, like a slow-rolling tear.

I found it funny because that was how I felt, like I was hanging off a cliff holding on for dear life, unable to tell up from down. My week had started out strange enough.

"Grace, you are so stubborn," he thrust his face toward the sky, raking his hands through his hair as he growled.

"I don't want to be with Abby; I want to be with you." He bit out forcefully as he looked to me begging me to forget what I had seen. Lightning flashed overhead, and thunder quickly followed. The raindrops slammed angrily down on us taking their frustration out on anything they could touch.

I jumped as the sound echoed, shuddering in my reply. "It didn't look that way to me. You seemed to be enjoying yourself immensely." I winced at the pain in my voice.

"No," he interrupted me again, shaking his head as his eyes grew round with shock.

"Is that what you really think of me? I don't know how she found out where we were tonight, but she did, and she played on you not being around. She said she just happened to be here and that I looked lonely. I tried to tell her to leave, that I was with someone. But she just plopped right down in the chair and picked up your menu like this was all normal. And then you walked out." Lightning crashed again striking somewhere close behind me.

He moved both warm hands to cup my cheeks and pull my face up toward his. Our noses mere centimeters apart. He looked me in the eyes making me watch as his silver irises swirled in the moonlight "Grace, it can't work with her. It never could have."

"Why not?" I whispered, pulling away and looking down at my borrowed shoes, letting my tears fall freely with the rain and my emotions get the better of me. I was tired of all the strangeness. I was beginning to think nothing in my life was real anymore. Too many strange activities in such a short period of time would do that to a person.

"Because I gave my heart away eleven years ago to the most beautiful girl I have ever met. From the moment she looked at me with those gorgeous green eyes, I was hers utterly and completely. I could never be anyone else's." The truth sparked behind his eyes as another bolt of lightning marred the night sky.

He wanted to kiss me; I could tell. I wanted to kiss him too, but this, none of this, was real. It couldn't be, because I'd wanted this for entirely too long.

"No." I shook my head and shoved away from him, swallowing the growing lump in my throat threatening to turn my tears in to heavy sobs. I looked in his eyes and saw pain sharp as a knife flash through them. I knew he couldn't possibly mean these words.

"You can't say those things to me," I chided and sniffled, needing him to understand that what he was saying couldn't be taken back, not with my heart so firmly in his hands. I tried to reign in my emotions. He really didn't need to see how his words affected me, how much I wanted to believe him, or how much I really did want him to kiss me.

"Why not?" he asked. I shook my head unable to express what I really wanted to say as I gulped in freezing air to cool my reactions. I really wanted to believe his words, but they only proceeded in driving and twisting the knife Abby had buried, even further through my heart.

He gave me a half grin and placed a tender kiss on my forehead. He pulled back. "Can I please take you home now?"

I shrugged. "I really want to tell you no, and that you blew it, but I'm soaked and turning into a Popsicle. So, I suppose you win."

"Good," he said as he pulled me along to the passenger side door and waited while I climbed in.

He handed me his jacket from the back seat and then we didn't talk again the entire ride home. I had nothing to say to him. Nothing that made sense anyways.

My emotions were all over the place. I wanted to believe him, that Abby's appearance at dinner was an accident, but at the same time, how could she have known where we'd be? Who was the stranger in the shadows? What was going on? Why was time pausing so much?

At home, I climbed the stairs, flicking off lights and locking doors all the way to my bathroom. I threw all my wet clothes including Eli's jacket into the tub. I had kicked my borrowed and ruined shoes off and left it all to lie where they fell.

I grabbed my warmest set of PJs and pulled my wet hair back in a knot, still feeling the cold damp air on my skin. I didn't want to think any more about what tonight meant. Too much had happened to even begin to decipher.

I found Evie and Lucky piled on my bed sound asleep and climbed up to join them. I hoped my dreams would make more sense than my reality did right then. Or at least provide an escape.

Tomorrow was Saturday, my first of many in the "in between"; everything would be clear tomorrow. It had to be.

But dreams wouldn't ease my blurry reality. There was no escape.

CHAPTER TWELVE

I was standing on a rocky cliff overlooking a vast and empty valley. A sliver of moonlight reflected off the tiny river below. My heart thundered in my chest. Footsteps crunched behind me, muffled and timid.

A murder of crows flew passed fleeing the approaching storm. I paused a moment to notice this was different and new. Warm sticky drops began to plop on the stones beneath my feet. The tall grass tickled my legs as the wind lifted my skirt. My hair whipped about against my face. "Grace," I heard whispered.

Surprised I looked over my shoulder, Eli stood reaching for me. His darkness oddly in contrast to his pale skin. His silver eyes glowed. "Please don't go, Grace," he pleaded. "If you jump, I'm coming after you," he spoke, his words echoing into the darkness.

I looked again to the encroaching storms turbulent and violent clouds. The blood began to pour from the clouds turning the river beneath me red. I looked over my shoulder at Eli and shook my head. "I must go. You cannot come with me. I must go alone." He stood reaching for my hand as if to pull me back, his heartbreak clear on his face.

I gave one last glance to him before I leapt off the ledge and down into the red river below.

I plunged into the water. My lungs seized as I surrendered to the current and it pulled me under.

My body was heaved into an enclosure, trapped in a cramped box void of all light. Thousands of haunting voices mocked and chanted at me. I was tortured so cruelly for hours until I no longer could tell the differences between them.

Invisible hands reached through make-believe walls and shook me, scratching and piercing anything for brief contact with my physical body. I felt isolated and alone in my own personal torment, held prisoner by unseen forces.

Then just as abruptly as it all started, it stopped. Blackness swallowed me whole; I was falling in a vacuum of nothingness, a new chant on repeat as the wind pushed and sucked me faster down.

"There is a garden enclosed, where a fountain is sealed,

that only the keeper of the vineyard may yield.

Unearthed to conceive the martyred prophets and angelic lives,

the descendants of prophesy and laws will survive.

Drawn from a garment to nurture ash into beauty.

To place upon each foot the burden of duality.

Drawing closer to one, deeper in love with another.

Training daily to slay as all innocence slips further.

The righteous gathered at the third watch of night,

Before the brazen alter of lava, among candlestick light.

The book of remembrance scribed on tablet in heart,

a sum of all patriarchs convened from each part.

The lord of host has sanctified a righteous seed,

from the throne of Heaven, a war was decreed.

Gathered winds in his fist, and wings lucent released,

to bond damnation in Hades and slay the beast."

Light exploded my vision; where there was dark now was light. Heat radiated from every pore in my body. I was glowing, ignited with knowledge and truth.

My back burned, but not a painful burn, a radiant burn. I felt my body soar higher instead of sinking. The wind pushed hard against me as I rose higher into consciousness. I heard singing, a chant I couldn't understand but could feel in my body, nonetheless. It was spiritual and full of love. I soared higher and higher and just as I thought I'd reached the surface, I rose higher.

I awoke slowly; sleep still clung to me like taffy. I yawned and stretched. My body felt new, my energy restored. I climbed out of bed, careful not to wake Evie. Lucky poked his little head up from under the covers, snorted, and crawled back under, turning his little nubby-tailed butt at me. Evie smiled and curled around him, still lost in dreamland.

I grabbed my clothes and gym bag. It was going to be a very long weekend. I tiptoed to the bathroom to brush my teeth and take my toothbrush with me. My clothes from last night still littered the floor, and like the flood, it all poured back into my memory. Emotions I didn't want to deal with lingered, but I pushed them down. I didn't have room in my head for all of that today.

I cleaned my mess, careful not to track water all over the floor on the way to the washer, clearing the evidence of my disastrous night.

I sent a quick text to Evie letting her know I'd be back later, though, honestly, I wasn't sure how long later would be. I was hoping before nightfall. I raced downstairs, trying not to be late and saw Lucas waiting for me in the driveway holding a strawberry smoothie.

"Day made!" I squealed.

He chuckled as I sucked down the pink deliciousness.

"Glad to see I still can have that effect on some girls."

"Uh oh, trouble in paradise?" I quizzed as I hopped into his rose-red Chevy pickup.

"Oh, only in the form of a hurricane," he sighed.

"Want to talk about it?"

"Nah, it's best I don't think about it. We broke up, end of story," he replied as he pushed his truck into reverse.

"I know the feeling," I muttered, as I tried to clear a strawberry stuck in my straw. Strawberry smoothies always had a way of perking me up. I wasn't sure if it was the color, the fruit, or the inherent sticky sweetness, but it worked.

He watched the road intently, but his eyes slanted every so often in my direction. I knew he wanted to know what had happened but didn't want to pry. They were best friends. I figured Eli would eventually tell him, which really was good, because I wasn't sure where to even start.

The drive from my house to headquarters wasn't long, and assuredly wasn't scenic, unless you liked dilapidated houses and dwellings that looked like they were constantly under construction. Without much delay, I could see the tops of the cathedral spires that marked the place in between.

We grabbed our bags and climbed the steps up to the double antique doors. The usual pressure pop feeling came over me just as we entered the door, marking the crossover between the realms. I'd never get used to the sights and feeling of entering another time and dimension.

Raguel greeted us at the door. "Welcome back, warriors," he enthused. "Lucas please see Grace to her room and give her the quick tour before we get started."

"This way." Lucas gestured for me to follow him up the enormous staircase.

The stairs up were long and tedious, something I doubted I'd ever grow used to. Lucas wasn't even winded by the time we made it all the way up to the living corridors. I, however, was gasping for air, trying desperately to suck enough into my lungs.

Lucas laughed and shook his head. "Come on, your room is at the end of the hall."

The long narrow hallway was dimly lit by shelled sconces. Sapphire and gold filigree carpet lined the floor. Almond-colored walls were warm and welcoming but only accentuated the fact that the hallway was extensive in its length.

My name was marked on the mahogany door by a little gold plaque.

"Come on in." Lucas gestured as he opened the door. I stopped dead in my tracks just inside. The room was almost an exact replica of mine at home.

I say almost because there was no Lucky lying on my bed waiting to greet me, and a new spare door was on the right wall beside the closet. In every other detail it was the same, right down to the scratch marks Mom had made on the closet doorjamb to mark my height growth through the years.

"How, is this possible?" I breathed in awe.

Lucas just shrugged and pulled his mouth into a tight-lipped smile.

"Is everyone's like this?"

"Pretty much, though I believe yours is larger than the rest of ours, and you have a separate bathroom, where the rest of us have to share with our neighbor."

"Isn't that awkward?"

"Nah, only sometimes, but for the most part it's like every other family with siblings."

"This is so surreal." I gasped.

Lucas just watched as I took the room in with stunned amazement. I was suddenly feeling like Alice falling down the rabbit's hole to another world. Surely my adventures wouldn't end the same.

I looked back at Lucas about to ask him when we were needed back downstairs, but when I turned, he was standing in the doorway, reminding me of an awkward bellhop at fancy hotels awaiting payment for his services.

He cleared his throat and looked down at his shoes. "Well, I'll leave you to explore your room." He looked up at me and a sadness had replaced his usual jovial expression. I had the distinct feeling he was hurt somehow. "Raguel wants us downstairs for orientation in about an hour." He turned his back to the room and grabbed the doorknob, lost inside himself. "My room is two doors down on the right if you need anything." He didn't wait for a reply as he shut the door.

I plopped down on my bed and closed my eyes, still in shock with the current state of my life. When did my life go from completely normal to this? I cleared my thoughts. Thinking about anything other than training wasn't going to help me in any form or fashion.

I quickly put away my packed bag and changed into workout gear. There were already a few items in my closet and my drawers, more workout gear and a few pairs of jeans and shirts. The tags were still on everything. Next, I went to explore my new home away from home.

Each door had ornate name plates hung with various personal touches. The door with Lucas's name on it was filled with baseball and football memorabilia, various pictures of the life he lived outside of GUESS quarters. My fingers brushed one of Lucas with Oliver, Eli, Evie, and me. It was newer than the others, but it seemed to stick out among the rest. This picture had just been taken yesterday for the yearbook. How did he get this picture? No one had seen it yet, except for the girl who took it.

My favorite picture was of the five of us from the fourth-grade Houston Zoo field trip. My ponytail and Evie's pigtails were on prominent display, as were Eli's braces.

I remember the day clearly. Lucas and Eli kept picking on Evie and me, much like they still did today. He had various pictures of people I'd never seen before. Each picture brought to light a new element I'd never seen in Lucas. I felt as if, after all these years, maybe I didn't really know him at all.

I turned to walk back down the hallway toward my room. I took notice of names and special touches on each room. Pieces of my faceless and nameless peers' lives outside of GUESS, real life people whom I'd be meeting soon, at least I hoped. The thought energized me with a skip of my heart. I hoped these people would like me. Meeting new people was not exactly something easily done for me. I made my way back to my room in no time. Again, I took notice of how blank my door was in comparison to the filled displays of the others. I would have to remedy that, and soon.

I had just sat down inside at my desk when Lucas knocked on my door. He smiled radiantly when I opened it. I took in what he was wearing, bare feet, tight black t-shirt, black training sweat pants, and a totally Lucas award-winning smile.

Despite the smile on his face, I couldn't help but feel as if there were a tight string between us about to snap. And I had no idea why. "Are you ready for this?" he asked. Breathless, I could only nod my head yes; internally I wasn't so confident. My training so far had been anything but successful. And that was without the audience I was about to have to perform in front of.

We arrived at an elevator bank I hadn't noticed on our way up. Lucas pushed the button for the floor we needed, and the doors popped right open. We rode down in vociferous silence. When the elevator dinged our arrival, I looked to Lucas who seemed lost in thought. A jaw muscle bulged with his frustration as he walked out and away from me before I could ask what it was that was bothering him. I trailed behind him all the way to the training ring.

"Nice of you two to join us," Raguel spat. Great, he was already in a wonderful mood. "Both of you to the front now." Lucas strode to Raguel in two steps, the crowd parting to let him through. I stood frozen to my spot.

I could feel too many eyes on me, whispers of disproval echoing in time to my thundering heartbeat. Lucas turned to face me, glaring at the people around us. I moved involuntarily following the tether tying me to him.

"Okay, Grace, Lucas," Raguel nodded to us both, "show us the basic defensive maneuvers." My mind drew a blank. I looked at Lucas, struck frozen. Lucas mouthed stop. I got into the stop position—palms up at eye level, elbows tucked in, with my dominant leg back. "Okay, which maneuver is she doing?" asked Raguel. A petite, cherub-faced girl raised her hand. "Yes, Li".

"Grace is showing us the stop maneuver."

"Great, Li, and what do we use this maneuver for?" Raguel asked.

Li replied, "It helps to position your body in order to target the soft spots, or rather pressure points, to stun or damage the attacker."

"Correct. Next," Raguel instructed, "where are the soft spots located?" This time a tall, dark-haired, lanky boy raised his hand. "Yes, Nasir" Raguel prompted.

Nasir smugly replied with a sneer on his face eyes locked with mine, "Eyes, nose, throat, chin, and groin."

"Perfect. Next show us the 360 defense with strike." Lucas faked like he was going to attack me from the front. I burst forward to block his hit with my forearm and aimed for his throat to disable him. His height hindered me from striking his eyes, so I had no choice but to strike at a lower soft spot. I didn't want to even pretend to hit below the belt, but it was sometimes necessary with the height difference between us.

"Good. Next position," was the only praise from Raguel I would get. I turned my back to Lucas and he went to attack in a bear hug grab from behind. I shifted my hips to the right, fake hit his groin with my palm, rotated, softly struck him in the neck with my elbow, and followed it up with a pretend kick to his groin.

Without prompting from Raguel we went on to the next maneuver. Lucas went to attack from behind me, grabbed my wrist to pull me toward him. In one fluid motion, I looked back at him, kicking him in the groin, rotated to face him, and hit him with a hammer fist to his neck.

It was an odd dance we had been practicing since the first day I had arrived there. We knew how to disarm and disable each other easily. Our display was met with applause from the crowd.

"Now, everyone break into pairs and practice these techniques. I'll let you know when to stop," Raguel boomed.

Everyone broke away and paired off. I felt every eye on me as they walked passed, some with more friendly expressions than others. Some glared hatefully. I suppose I didn't live up to their expectations either. It was a feeling I was becoming exceptionally used to. Lucas touched my shoulder and I nearly jumped out of my skin. "Hey, let's get to work. Raguel seems moodier than usual."

True to form, Raguel let us torture ourselves until we were all so tired, we could fall down. It felt like hours later when he called us to break for lunch. Lucas gestured for me to follow him to the cafeteria. I shook my head. "I'm not really hungry; I'll just practice more while you guys take a break." Lucas seemed puzzled over my decline of food.

"Grace, come on, you need to eat and rest."

I shook my head again and looked at the floor. "Lucas, I can't face them right now. I can't face myself right now. I can't go in there and be who they want me to be. You heard what they said about me. You saw the response I got from them."

Lucas stepped closer to me and pulled my chin up to look him in the eyes. "That is not the words the Grace I know would say." Lucas chuckled. "In fact, the Grace I know would march her happy butt into that room and charm them all with her smile and sass. And probably have a few sandwiches gone before anyone else had a turn at the food line."

I pulled away. "I'm not that Grace anymore." I heaved a breathless sigh. "I don't exactly know who I am anymore." I turned away from Lucas to face the mirror, afraid of what my reflection would show.

I looked at Lucas in the mirror too afraid of looking at myself. He looked as if he wanted to say something, but instead he hung his head and walked away, lost in his own thoughts.

I drilled myself until I couldn't stand anymore and lay down on the mat to catch my breath. I stayed that way until lunch was over. People began to gather again in a half circle looking refreshed and ready for more sparing. I personally felt like I needed a shower and a long nap.

Lucas helped me up from the mat and we took our places in the half circle. Raguel announced, "Calisthenics for the rest of the day," and turned in a flourished huff to stand watch over us like a lord overseer. This part always had me sucking pond water. I was not completely out of shape, but I didn't tend to do much exercising outside of PE. Everyone paired off doing pushups, sit-ups, burpees, and lunges in perfect, synchronized rhythm.

Lucas paired with me as if on autopilot. "You don't have to babysit me, Lucas. There are plenty of other people you can pair off with, people who are highly skilled, to which I am the opposite."

He looked taken back by my declaration. "It's not like that, Grace." He seemed to think about his response. "You and I are partners." As if that made all the sense in the world and was the only explanation needed. "Well, I'll talk to Raguel about that. I don't want to hold you back from training."

None of this was routine for me. I had to take cues from the pairs surrounding me to know what was next in the routine. Lucas didn't speak to me anymore, not even words of encouragement to keep me motivated. It was okay, though, because I really had nothing to say. I was dealing with too many weird situations and too many unanswered questions to talk to anyone.

When the time came to run, we all took off at a decent trot. Apparently, that was not the normal pace because without notice everyone sped up. That is, everyone but me. With each passing lap, I fell further and further behind. At one point, I was lapped fully twice by the entire group. I kept my head up and focused, but I could feel their dissatisfaction and disproval of me.

The third time I was lapped, they didn't go around me; instead, they swarmed me in a mass of sweaty bodies shoving and elbowing me on their way by. "Hurry up," someone exclaimed. "Pathetic," spat another. Before it was over, someone stuck their foot in front of mine, tripped me, and I landed with a hard thump on the wooden floor. I skinned my knee, both my palms, and had a rub burn on my chin. Lucas stopped to help me up. I reluctantly accepted the help.

Raguel blew the whistle, which made everyone stop. "Who did that?" he boomed. He walked down the stairs of his perch and proceeded to interrogate the others. "Grace, you are dismissed. Go get cleaned up and rest before dinner." I turned and went up the stairs to my room. My pride was more bruised than my body.

CHAPTER THIRTEEN

I sat at my desk playing with the little black box with the pink bow. I admit I was curious as to what was inside, but I didn't want the rug to be pulled out from under me again, so I was hesitant to open it. I was a bit afraid that whatever was inside would bite me. That kind of thing had been my luck lately. I didn't want to go to dinner with everyone else today. I wanted to be alone in my thoughts. I wanted to work through my ever-growing list of questions. I'd rather have eaten in my room, but I couldn't ignore the knock at my door.

I plopped the box back down on the desk and dragged myself over to the door to open it. "What?" I asked in a huff. "Oh, Raguel, I'm sorry I thought it would be someone else."

Raguel cleared his throat and raised an eyebrow. "Like Lucas?" he teased.

I rolled my eyes at his tone. "No," was my only reply.

He gestured to the door. "I'm here to escort you safely to dinner."

"I'm really not hungry." I shook my head to decline, eyeing the box I had just set down.

Raguel followed my gaze then looked back up at me. "You still haven't opened it?" He looked stunned. I shook my head no. "Would you like me to open it for you?" he probed.

"No," I replied dryly again. He seemed put off by my lack of acceptance of his present, like he was personally hurt by my not wanting the gift. It was odd, but what wasn't odd anymore?

He picked up the tiny box turning it over in his hands, seemingly lost in thought. "This was a gift from your father.

It's a family heirloom." He looked up to meet my eyes as he gently set the box back down.

Gesturing once again to the door, he repeated, "Unfortunately for you, dinner is mandatory; and seeing as how you did not eat lunch, you need to eat dinner. Now let's go." I sighed and hung my head as I followed him out the door and into the dining hall.

The dining hall was like nothing that I had imagined. I expected it to be more like the school's cafeteria than the grand formal dining room that it was. The awe-inspiring length of the burnished oak table took up most of the space in the room. Hundreds of cream plush dining chairs sat regally against the table.

Elegant tapestries depicting scenes from angelic history hung from braided metal cords to cover the dark wooden walls. The floor was covered in a plush emerald dyed rug; only the outer edges of the wooden floor beneath could be seen. The room was lit within from thousands of candlesticks upon brass hanging candelabras.

The room was already full to bursting. The chatting and laughter from my fellow students suddenly stopped as we entered the room. I felt every soul gaze upon me as the hush fell over the crowd. I was seated at the furthest seat from the heavy doors that led into the hall. They were propped open with door stops made from golden lion-headed statues. Lucas was on my right, and, to my surprise, Raguel took the seat on my left. No one spoke a word.

The soundless pressure began to build in my eardrums until I was sure they would burst. Servers brought out plates of roasted chicken, steamed vegetables, and cloud-like rolls with heaps of butter. A plate was set before each of us.

I could hear the clank and clatter of every served item. It set my nerves on edge. I clamped my teeth to keep from speaking, yet still no one else spoke. A crystal goblet filled with water was set before me. I busied myself with pretending I was eating while listening to the scrapes of silverware on porcelain plates. It was like nails on a chalkboard.

The sounds made me want to scream. With the loathing eyes and the sounds of our dinner being consumed, it took every ounce of self-control I had not to remove myself from the table.

Eventually, I tried to eat. But I only ended up pushing my food around my plate as I sat in anguish. Dinner seemed to take years. I could feel each second ticking by, drawing out the torture further. I watched as some picked at their food with their fingers and sucked it off with a loud smack. It made me squirm.

As soon as I politely could, I made a heroic attempt to excuse myself from the table. I even tried to forgo the delectable chocolate cake that was served for dessert, but Raguel wouldn't let me be excused, just shaking his head at my feeble, whispered attempts to be dismissed.

When the last of the plates were cleared, everyone stood and left the dining hall as one. Everyone but the three of us in my corner of the table that is. Raguel dismissed Lucas and me with a scorning wave of his hand. I walked with Lucas to the double doors and then made my escape alone. He made a move like he was going to follow me but met my eyes and then hung his head, turned, and walked in the opposite direction, leaving me alone.

I wandered the halls of GUESS headquarters alone, lost in my thoughts. Dinner was awful. Not the food; that part was admittedly delicious, what I had tasted of it anyway. It was just the atmosphere.

I missed my simple dinners with Mom and Lucky. I missed the way my mother would ask about my day, smiling to showcase her thin, crinkled smile lines and tiny crow's feet in the corners of her eyes and the way she freely laughed at any random thing I would say.

I walked past more doors with nameplates and pictures. I didn't bother looking to see who they were, as I no longer wished to be a part of these people. I felt like an outcast. I walked past the training facility to the grand staircase that led up to my landing. When I finally made it up to my room again, I closed and locked the door.

Leaning against it, I sighed heavily and sank to my bottom on the floor, as silent tears bloomed in my eyes. My body began to tremble as I drank in huge gulps of air. Soon it was overwhelming, and I shook with rage and anguish as the tears were released to plunge down my cheeks in waterfall-like waves. A knock reverberated through the room. I didn't answer. I was determined not to open the door until the following morning. Whatever and whoever it was could wait.

I refused to wallow anymore in disappointment. I scrubbed my hands over my eyes to remove the traces of tears and climbed up from the floor. I stood and reached for the little black box on my desk. I sat on the edge of the bed and untied the bow, letting the pink ribbon fall to the floor before I could change my mind again.

Lifting the lid of the box, I closed my eyes trying to prepare myself for what I would see. When I finally scrounged up enough courage to look, I saw that inside the box lay a necklace made of braided silver.

The pendant that hung on it was a solid silver cross woven to sharp points at each tip. Diamond angel wings in flight extended from the center of the cross and out past each point of the patibulum. It looked like sheets of glass extended from the cross itself. I knew they were real diamonds though because of the way the light refracted and bounced rainbows of colors through them.

The pendant was attached to the chain at the uppermost point of the stipe. All in all, the pendant was only a couple of inches in width and length. It was heavy, yet it seemed delicate and fragile.

I carefully lifted it from the box and clasped it around my neck. It settled into my chest, longer than most necklaces but not long enough that it hit my navel. The weight of it felt right, as if it were made for me and not a man. I shook my head, not just any man, my father. A family heirloom from a forbidden branch I would never know. It held a comforting warmth, like an embrace from a loving parent.

I lay back and curled in a ball trying fruitlessly to go to sleep. My hand unconsciously rested over the necklace. My mind whirled with everything that had happened. There was no making sense of it. I was resigned to my fate. This is what life would be like for me now. Small teenage drama and insubstantial problems were long gone and in their place was a boulder of truth. I no longer had a choice; I had to become the person the world needed me to be. That intensity alone bore its own heavy certainty.

Sleep was futile. After what seemed like hours of tossing and turning and trying to surrender to the siren's call of sleep, I instead surrendered to my pent-up frustration and whipped my sheets back to climb out of bed. I threw on a quick set of training clothes and decided to work out my frustrations. As quietly as I could, I made my way down to the training arena.

I'm not sure what I expected to find or who I expected to be down there, but the room was surprisingly empty. I made my way down the stairs and stopped on the huge blue mat in front of the mirror.

It reminded me of when I took baton twirling lessons as a little girl. That was a long time ago, though, and I don't remember much from classes. A distant memory flashed in my mind of a recital.

I remembered wearing a pink costume with rhinestones all over catching the lights when I moved. It had a tiny sheer skirt that was made of teardrop-shaped pieces of thin material that curled at the edges. I dropped the baton many times, but as we took our bow on stage, my mom was clapping as if it were an award-winning performance. I smiled a little despite all the chaos in my heart.

I had begun to stretch and warm up my muscles when I heard a rustle of clothing behind me. Raguel had found me. "I couldn't sleep," was all I said to him as a way of greeting. It felt like explanation enough. I didn't want company, but here he was anyway.

He nodded and tossed me a wooden practice sword. I reached up and caught it out of reflex, surprising us both when I did. "What's this?" I asked, gesturing to the sword I was holding in one hand.

"A practice sword," he replied dryly.

"I know that, but what do you want me to do with it?" I shrugged in a huff.

He nodded seeming to understand some of my confusion. "Right. Sword fighting always helps wear me down enough to sleep."

"I don't know how to sword fight." My voice rose an octave with the uncertainty of it.

I held the heavy wooden sword in my hands. It was small and looked more like a toy than an actual practice weapon. I doubted any real swords would be this small. "You're holding it wrong."

I rolled my eyes. Of course, I was. It was fitting since I seemingly couldn't do anything correctly. "I told you I have no idea what I'm doing."

He let out a frustrated breath. "First take your forward hand and grip it like you would a handshake. With your rear hand, grip the same but push your hands together," he coached, showing me with his hands as he went through the instruction.

"Like this?" I asked.

He nodded his head. "Now, stand with your feet a comfortable distance apart. You want to make sure you are steady on your feet and not easily knocked over, yet free to move."

I positioned myself like he said, hoping it was right.

"Now, when you go to strike, you'll be striking across your body. Right to left or left to right." He moved the sword in slashing motions. "When you move your right or front foot forward, you're lunging for attack; when you move it back, it's called a burst. When you move, it should just come quite naturally." He progressed in front of me and readied himself. "You attack first." He signaled.

I moved to swing the heavy sword, but he back-stepped out of the way. "Too slow. You don't want me to know what you're about to do. You have to move your body faster and not project where you're about to strike." I took a deep breath trying hard not to lose my patience. I really did want to learn to do just one thing right.

I tried again, this time moving faster, but he still blocked my swing with a thrust of his own that sent shock waves down my arms with jolting electric pain. "Ouch!" I dropped the sword with a thud and swung my arms wildly to get the blood flowing back into them.

"Pick up the sword, Grace." Raguel roared, growing more irritated with my inferiority.

"Give me a second," I said, still swinging my arms around nervously. About that time, I went air born falling backwards flat onto my back with a hard thud. All the breath was knocked out of my lungs, and my necklace smacked me in the face hard enough to sting.

"Your father would be disappointed. You aren't even trying," he boomed, looking straight at the necklace on my face.

"I am trying," I bit out with bitter resentment.

"No, you aren't. All of this should be as natural as breathing to you. It doesn't have to be hard. You are making it hard." His muscular jaw clinched and unclenched.

He waved his hand indicating to encompass all of me as he growled his frustration. "This is your choice. You have the power to do all of this and more. You have any ability you choose, yet you choose none."

I just sat mouth agape while he raged away. Words failed me in my time of fury.

"Why are you even here if you don't want to learn to use your power?" He shook his head and continued his tirade. "You shouldn't be here, and you shouldn't be wearing that necklace." He pointed at my face where the necklace lay before continuing his outburst. "I should have never given it to you until I knew you were ready." He turned his back to walk away.

Pure white-hot rage boiled beneath my skin. I was scorching, so fiery hot, I could painfully feel the waves of anger and frustration radiating off me. The necklace burned my fevered skin.

I was tired of being a disappointment to myself and to everyone else. I was tired of never being good enough. I was tired of the secrecy and lies I had to tell. I was tired of this place, these people, all of it. I wanted to go home.

I was shaking with so much bubbling anger threatening to spew out of me like some warped volcano. "Fine!" I screamed. "I'm done." I couldn't take any more of this helpless feeling. "If I'm such a disappointment to all of you, I'll leave." Flatly trying to keep as much of a cool head as I could at this point, I sat up to face him again. "Oh, and Raguel, here." Rising to my feet, I went to grab the necklace, ripped it off me, and threw it at his face. But when the clasp broke free from my neck, a concussive sonic boom exploded from it.

It shook the entire foundation of the building, sending shockwaves out in its wake. My ears began to ring loudly. Time stalled.

Just before the chain could completely leave my hand, light exploded all around me, similar to what I saw the first time I had ever laid eyes on Raguel's true form. But this wasn't from Raguel. This light was coming from the necklace.

The chain wrapped itself around my arm forming a gauntlet of chain. Blindingly brilliant light erupted from the cross itself, reforming and molding in front of my eyes.

I could feel it taking shape in my hand. A dazzling magnificent sword made of glittering light took the place of the cross. The diamond wings wrapped around my hand as a sort of hand guard on the hilt of the sword, protectively covering them, bending and refracting the light in tiny rainbows all around me. The sword was so lightweight it practically felt like air.

It suddenly became a part of me, like my lungs or my heart. I could feel it reading me, my emotions, my feelings, my mind. I could feel it bury itself into my head learning how my brain worked.

When it opened my memories, people's faces flashed in front of my eyes, and I knew their names and each emotion they created within me. It reached as far back as it could, to my birth, learning my life as if it were its own.

Then it began to pour its own knowledge into me. Reforming what I knew of combat fighting and war, feeding me what it knew in their place. It agonizingly pushed my muscles into new muscle memories, fighting positions for almost every type of combat known to man and some only known to the angelic, reaching some unknown part within me. It poured light into every nerve ending in my body, burning away all that it felt I no longer needed. I was made anew.

I returned to myself, flat on my back. I gasped, staring up at a laughing Raguel, a worried Lucas, and all my classmates who had awoken from their sleep to see the commotion. I tried to sit up, still clutching the sword. I pulled it in front of my face not actually believing it was real. I looked around the room trying to make out the hushed conversations, but something drew my eye to the windows.

I could see shadowy figures moving, ebbing and flowing in the inky-black darkness. "What is that?" I whispered fearfully.

Raguel looked where I was pointing and stated, "That is the darkness. It's always there. Darkness wants what it can't have. Though there are more of them out there tonight. Your light must have drawn them here."

My eyes rounded like saucers. "Can they get in?"

"No," Lucas interrupted as he helped me get to my feet, carefully avoiding the sword still molded in my hand. Rubbing my shoulders, he gently asked, "Are you okay?"

Not trusting my words, I just nodded my head. Okay was a relative term anyway. I felt energized, renewed. I was more than okay, but also a little more than confused.

Raguel jovially clapped his hands together. "Okay, Grace, let's see what you can do with that flaming sword." He attacked, suddenly sending Lucas diving swiftly out of the way. Light blazed from the sword. I blocked the attack. I feinted right, Raguel moved to block, but I struck left, slicing a nick in his pristine white shirt precisely at his rib cage. I should have seen blood because the sword told me we had struck him true.

He struck out again, this time aiming toward my feet. I stepped back and blocked, twirled around, and sliced with my left hand. Raguel leaped and spun in the air arcing his sword to slice me in half. I moved to circle parry his sword out of his hand, sending the wooden sword airborne and away from his reaching distance. I watched his sword as it flew out of his hands and landed hilt up, point stuck in the bottom step of the grand staircase. I had him dead to rights. The room erupted in applause and cheers. Raguel smiled brilliantly. He seemed proud.

The rest of training went just like that. I no longer was at the back of the pack when we ran. Now I led the run. I no longer was exhausted before lunch; instead, I'd barely even break a sweat. The sword and I knew each fighting maneuver my opponent would try defending, striking and disabling with whatever weapon we used before it was in motion. I still felt like an outcast, but now it wasn't because I was performing poorly. It was because no one could beat me.

Lucas was the only one who would still spar with me. Raguel spent the evenings helping me learn to call the sword and how to make it retract when it was no longer needed. He seemed relaxed and happy with himself, a far cry from the bitter anger he had clung onto when he first started training me.

During one of our evening lessons, he explained that Cherubim, a class of angels, was put at the gates of the Garden of Eden to guard it when God cast Adam out of it. Flaming swords blocked the entry.

My sword was likened to those ancient swords—separate entities, yet tools only the angelic could use. That revelation left me dumbfounded. The knowledge that the sword was alive made me shiver. But I knew this was true.

From the day I first called my sword, I finally felt as if I could do this. I could be the one to save the world. For the first time, I believed in myself. I just had to find the prophet and law giver before it was too late.

CHAPTER FOURTEEN

The last day of training was met with sorrow from several of the GUESS members. They had formed lifelong friendships that they would leave behind to continue their human lives until it was time for them to fight. Training wasn't new to them like it was me. That weight squeezed my heart like an iron fist. I hadn't made friends there. This was the first and only time I would train with them as a group.

The few members who talked with me did so with no more detail than polite conversation when necessary. Far better than where I had started, but it saddened me because I still didn't feel like I belonged.

The last night there we had a dance and party as a celebration for my coming into my powers and to, supposedly, solidify our growth as a community. I was pretty much a social outcast in real everyday life and only stuck with our small group of friends. It worked for us in the real world, but there I had only Lucas; and even that friendship seemed strained lately.

Since the required attire that evening was semi-formal, I dressed in the only dress I had that would work with the evening's dress code, my dress for the homecoming dance. I hadn't yet worn it because homecoming was still a week away.

I bought it with hopes that Eli would ask me to be his date for the dance. That wish seemed pointless now considering our recent disastrous date. My dress was a short, tight-fitting cream color that ended at the knee. Bunched from the hips to leave the front of the dress open at the waist and flaring to the ground, was a sheer, golden skirt that made a semi-train. The halter neckline had shimmering, tiny golden beads. I wore gold strappy heels and my hair half up, leaving the cross necklace on prominent display. I scrounged up as much courage as I could and left to enjoy the party.

As I made my way down to the training area, I saw Lucas waiting for me at the bottom of the staircase. He lifted his eyes up and sucked in a breath as if someone had knocked the air out him when he saw me. I stopped two steps from the bottom, which made us close to eye level. I could feel his burning gaze rake over me as if he were really seeing me for the first time. He looked refined and handsome in his black tux.

He finally raised his eyes to meet mine and gave me one of his best dazzling smiles as he raked his hand through his tousled blonde hair. "Hello, beautiful." He cleared his throat and looked absently away. "I thought I'd escort you to the ballroom if that's okay with you." I felt a bit timid but nodded my head yes and took his hand to descend the last two steps. Lucas was my friend after all. I hooked my arm in his and walked with him toward the ballroom.

The party had already started, and crowds of people were already dancing to the thumping beat of the music. The noise hit me with a crashing wave of sound after the near silence from the rest of the headquarters. Lucas was stopped by a horde of girls just inside the door, so I made my way over to the punch table. Clear bubbling liquid was in the punch bowl, and hundreds of real crystal champagne flutes lined the pristine, white linen tablecloth.

I took one of the flutes and filled it with the punch. The bubbles burned their way down my throat. Sparkling grape soda. I watched as it made the glass fog with condensation. I made my way to a darker corner of the room to sit out and watch the cheerful dancers as they bounced about on the dance floor.

It made me happy to see everyone enjoying themselves, but I couldn't help the pang of sadness that washed over me in a suffocating wave. After a few songs, I noticed the beat changed to a slow song. Dancers paired off, two by two, rocking with the rhythm the music played.

Raguel suddenly appeared beside me seemingly out of nowhere. "Would you care to dance?" He seemed unsure that I would accept. He wasn't wrong. Every instinct in me told me to tell him no. It wasn't that I didn't like him as a person; it was that we just clashed awkwardly like only two entirely different species could, neither seeing or understanding what the other was seeing. I hesitated before setting my flute of soda down and taking his offered hand. He visibly relaxed at my acceptance.

He escorted me to the middle of the dance floor, the crowd parting before us. He held my right hand enveloped in his large calloused one. The other lightly sat on my hip. I rested my other hand on his arm as we began to sway to the music.

After a few turns everyone relaxed back into motion. "Grace..." Raguel seemed to stumble over his words. "...I know I was hard on you, and you probably do not like me very much. But I wanted you to know that I am proud of you." He shook his head. "I shouldn't have said that you didn't belong here or that I shouldn't have given you the necklace." He cast his eyes to the floor.

I sighed and patted his arm. "We said a lot of things to each other we shouldn't have."

He looked up to meet my eyes and smiled, chuckling to himself. "You're as fiery tempered as your father, but also kind and diplomatic like your mother." He twirled me around and I couldn't help the giggle fit I let loose. It was pure joy. I felt like a little girl again in that moment. Part of me still was that little girl, but part of me was somewhere more grown up and cynical.

When the song ended, Raguel bowed and I held my skirt and curtsied. He chuckled, his voice booming over the last strains of music. After that dance, it seemed to relax the rest of the people, and I soon found my dance card filled to bursting.

I met Emeka from Swahili. He had ebony-colored skin with the darkest eyes I'd ever seen in a human. His hair was shaved except for a small circular tuft at the back of his head. He had a piercing in his left ear, a copper cuff. Intricate dots and lines marked his exposed skin. He wore the traditional African Dashiki in bold vibrant reds, blues, and yellows. He was sweet and had the kindest smile.

Next, I danced with Nasir, followed by his identical twin brother, Rami, from Iran. I couldn't tell them apart, both tall and lanky with a day's worth of facial hair growth on their chins.

Then I was dancing with Cheng. He was taller than I, but shorter than most of the boys there. His dance moves were smooth and graceful compared to the other boys. I excused myself to take a break, my shoes beginning to wear my feet out.

As soon as I sat, four girls came chatting and giggling up to me to introduce themselves. First was Nara. She had blue eyes, like an ocean, with fiery red hair. Her Irish accent was divine and made me laugh at some of her euphemisms. Alyona was from Russia, and I learned she had a life-sized crush on Nasir. Jess was stunning with her sky-blue eyes, curly black hair, and full plush lips. Last, Li introduced herself. Li had a beautiful cherub face. She reminded me of a doll all dainty and petite.

"How do you know Lucas?" Jess probed.

"I grew up with him. He's my best friend's brother's best friend." I wrinkled my nose unsure if that made sense. He was more than just a friend of a friend, but it seemed too complicated to explain.

The girls went on chatting about all the boys at GUESS. I soon tuned them out. Girl talk wasn't the same without Evie. I found myself missing her more and more.

Lucas cleared his throat. "Dance with me, Grace." It wasn't a question. He took my hand and pulled me to my feet rushing me to the dance floor. "You looked lost; I thought I'd come rescue you," he joked. His smile lit up his whole face. I realized he didn't smile as often as he used to and found myself wishing I could help him with whatever was bothering him.

We were dancing to an upbeat song from another country. I couldn't understand the words, but the beat of the music was fast and happy. All the dancers on the floor were doing the same movements in time to the music. We joined in, hopping and shimmying in unison. Heel-toe-hop, heel-toe-hop. Dance around your partner. Switch. We repeated the steps with new partners until we were back together again. It was a happy and freeing dance, and for the first time there, I was enjoying being in the moment.

The music switched to a slow song. Lucas only hesitated a second before pulling me to him, settling both of his hands at my waist. Unlike with Raguel, we danced close and informally. It wasn't our first time to slow dance together, but it suddenly had my heart beating faster in my chest at the closeness and familiarity we shared. "Lucas, you know you can talk to me about anything, right?" I couldn't help but ask. I knew in my heart something was eating at him.

He tensed under my hands and looked away unable to meet my gaze. "Yeah, but the same goes for you. You can talk to me about anything." I shook my head and let it go.

Soon I found myself putting my head on his chest. He sighed and pulled me closer, resting his chin on top of my head. We stayed that way for a few songs before I excused myself to my room for the night. As soon as I made it to the hall just outside the ballroom, I kicked my shoes off and carried them the rest of the way up the stairs.

Sleep greeted me like a long-lost old friend. I didn't dream that night. I awoke the next morning with a smile still on my face. I packed in a hurry, ready to be home. I hugged the few people who had made an effort to be my friend vowing we'd talk again soon. I gave them all my Skype ID and my phone number to text, in hopes of securing our friendships.

I spotted Raguel by the door and leapt up to hug him. He seemed shocked but accepted my hug with a hug of his own wrapping his large arms around me. I said, "Thank you," trying to express my gratitude for his help and his long-suffering training. He pushed me to be the best I could be, and, in the end, it was he who helped me the most.

He reluctantly set me back down and kissed the top of my head. "See you soon, Grace."

Lucas took my bag from my hands and moved to the doors. "Ready to go home?"

I nodded and pushed the door open.

Sunlight burst before my eyes, warming my face. I hadn't been outside in the last few weeks of training at the GUESS headquarters. I smiled and tilted my head to the sun before getting into Lucas's truck. The clock on the dashboard read 10:00 a.m., the same morning we had left out for training all those many weeks ago. I'd never get used to this time difference.

Before I knew it, we were home. I walked inside and sat my bag by the door. Lucas walked in with me. Mom was at the kitchen counter making a fruit salad. "Hey, you guys hungry?"

Lucas took a seat next to me at the bar. "Starving."

I playfully punched his arm. "You are always starving." Mom smiled and scooped out four bowls of fruit salad. She moved around the bar and gave me a kiss on the cheek. "So, how was it?" Before I could answer her, I heard Lucky and Evie racing down the stairs. I guess our conversation would have to wait.

CHAPTER FIFTEEN

"Beach day!" Evie squealed before taking the other seat next to me and plopping a fat red strawberry into her mouth.

Lucas and I watched her with confused expressions. "Beach day?"

Evie rolled her eyes. "When you were in the bathroom, Eli sent out a group text and asked everyone if we wanted to go to the beach." At that time, both Lucas's and my cellphones chimed the text. We met each other's eyes before Lucas turned to read his and started typing out a response. "Oliver is going; that leaves us three." He took a bite of his fruit salad and wagged his eyebrows at me. "Beach day?"

I nodded my head and sighed, "Yeah, sounds good. Beach day it is." I looked at my mom to see if it was okay, but she had this smile plastered on her face and was staring off into space. We finished our fruit salad while Evie talked nonstop about Abby and Ashley and all the trivial teenage things I had forgotten about.

When we were done, I cleaned up the dishes while Evie and Lucas went home to change and grab their beach stuff. Evie hollered on her way out the door that she'd be back in ten minutes. "Mom." I hesitated a moment. She seemed to suddenly snap out of it.

"Yeah, honey." She finally looked up at me acknowledging I was truly there with her.

"Evie, Eli, Lucas, and Oliver are going to the beach today and would like to know if I can go with them." I raised my eyebrows in question.

She seemed to think for a moment. "Sure, that sounds like fun. I have to go into work today, so I won't be here when you get back. But promise me you'll tell me all about training when I get home tomorrow morning."

I smiled and said, "It's a date."

I grabbed my bag and raced up the stairs for a quick change. I flipped my hair into a ponytail and threw on my bathing suit, a simple black one-piece that had a deep v neckline and embroidered belt just under the bust. I slipped some cut off jean shorts and a bright pink tank top over the top, slid on my flip-flops, and grabbed a towel and some sunscreen. As an afterthought, I threw in a change of clothes and my brush before rushing back down the stairs. I kissed my mom on the cheek and patted Lucky just as Evie knocked.

Evie raced me back to her brother's car and hopped in the backseat before I could protest. I still wasn't ready to face whatever was happening between Eli and me, but Evie was persistent.

We had about a forty-five-minute drive until we hit the beach, and I was about to have to endure it in the front seat next to my long-time crush and the person who broke my heart just days ago. I sighed and buckled in. We made our way down to Galveston with the windows down, sunglasses on, and singing along to the loud music playing over the speakers.

Galveston, Texas, was an island city on the Gulf of Mexico. It had it all. Galveston was home to miles of sandy beaches continuing over a ferry boat to Bolivar Peninsula.

Additionally, Galveston, was home to an enchanting historic district filled with wonderful little shops. My favorite was the Confectionery, which had handmade chocolates, to die for salt-water taffy, and an old-fashioned soda fountain.

The island was also home to an amusement park, museums of which some were inside glass pyramids, loads of beachside shops, heaps of different style restaurants, and even a cruise port. Every summer break, hordes of people flooded the island due to its various attractions.

Luckily for us, prime beach-going season was ending since Texas public schools were back in session. It was close to lunch by the time we made it to the Seawall, so we stopped at a drive-through on our way out. We pulled up to our favorite beach just in time to see Oliver and Lucas pull out the beach umbrella and a cooler full of soft drinks.

Eli parked next to Lucas's truck and turned the car off. I hopped out to greet Ollie and Lucas before Eli had the chance to stop me, if he even was. I was not going to let our bad date ruin our fun today.

I playfully punched Lucas and Ollie in the arms as a way of greeting. Evie was glaring at Eli who looked dumbstruck when I finally turned to look at him. I pulled my towel and sunscreen out of my bag and laid out my spot just outside of the sun's reach. I took off my flip-flops to feel the dry warm sand between my toes.

I tended to burn easily so sunscreen was always a must. I threw off my shorts and tank top and began slathering the white oily sunscreen all over the exposed parts of me. Mom wouldn't be happy if I burned, and I surely didn't want that pain.

Evie dropped her bag next to mine and began smoothing out her towel. Eli tossed his shirt hitting me in the face on his way by. Evie and I about died laughing; his aim was always astonishingly accurate. The guys began throwing a frisbee in ankle deep water, when Evie turned to me and asked the question I'd been dreading since I'd last seen her.

"So, how'd the date go?"

I sighed and prepared to tell my long agonizing tale of woe. "It didn't."

She sucked in a sharp breath. "What did he do?"

I shook my head to deter her anger at her brother. "It wasn't all him. Abby was there." Evie's eyes went wide as saucers. "I don't think he invited her..." I paused sensing for the first time that maybe he was telling the truth. "... He says he doesn't know how she found out where we would be. But there she was in my seat anyway." I didn't tell her about the strange darkness or the weird electricity between Eli and me.

I drew in a breath with courage enough to tell her what I felt I could without violating Eli's trust. "It was raining when we got to the restaurant. All your hard work was undone. I excused myself to the restroom to try and fix myself back up. When I came back out of the bathroom, I saw her sitting in my empty chair. They looked happy and content. I didn't want to bother them, so I left. He followed me out to the car and drove me home. End of story." I looked out at the guys who had moved on to touch football, tossing the ball in the air and running down the coast line while the other two tried to tackle the one with the ball, completely against touch football rules.

I didn't want to see the disappointment on Evie's face. Eli had the ball now and was running back our direction as fast as he could, looking over his shoulder to dodge a swipe from Lucas. Oliver was left way behind, unable to keep up with their fast pace. Just before Eli got to us at the shore line, Lucas tackled him, sending a huge splash of water to land at our feet. We all cracked up laughing.

"Want to go for a walk?" I asked Evie to break the spell of my tale of woe.

She beamed at me. "I thought you'd never ask." We linked arms and walked away down the coast looking for sand dollars and seashells. After a while we turned and made our way back to the umbrella and the guys. Evie handed me her collected treasure. "Can you put this in my bag? I'm going to teach these guys a thing or two about how to play football."

I laughed until I snorted. "Sure."

I bent to unzip a pocket on my backpack and pulled out my book, emptying my accumulated shells into the pocket in its place. I grabbed Evie's bag and drug it to me. Evie didn't have a large pocket on the front of her backpack, so I unzipped the main compartment and settled her keepsakes inside, accidentally knocking out a piece of folded notebook paper.

I picked it up to put it back, but it shocked me—the same zinging kind of electric shock I felt when I touched Raguel for the first time. The paper glowed a strange golden light, just like my sword. I sucked in a sharp breath. I needed to see what was on that piece of paper. Whatever it was, I knew I needed to read it, that it had something to do with me. But why did Evie have it?

I glanced up to see where Evie was and saw her playing football with the guys, splashing water at anyone who dared come near her. Their boisterous laughter filled the air. I hesitated a moment before opening the piece of paper, afraid I'd betray Evie's trust. That knot of anxiety and fear sank in my heart like a boulder to the bottom of an ocean. I knew in my bones this was meant for me. It was confirmed the moment I read what Evie had scrawled in her large and loopy handwriting.

"There is a garden enclosed, where a fountain is sealed

That only the keeper of the vineyard may yield.

Unearthed to conceive the martyred prophets and angelic

lives,

The descendants of prophesy and laws will survive."

The words to my dream were written on this paper. But why would Evie have this? How would she know about this because I hadn't told anyone? The answer was staring me in the face as Evie and the guys made their way back to me and the shade of the umbrella.

My heart tore in two. My vision blurred white. I could feel my pulse pounding as if my heart were trying to escape its prison inside my chest. Evie was the prophet. That dawning realization burned in my soul. I quickly folded the piece of paper back up and stuffed it back into a small side pocket of

Evie's bag before they all fell down beside me in a fit of laughter.

I must have worn a strange expression because Lucas looked at me and mouthed, "Are you okay?"

I shook my head no and mouthed back, "Later."

Eli watched our exchange with burning furry. Tension between us constricted with a different kind of ache in my heart. It wasn't lost on him that Lucas and I had become closer, though he didn't know the why of it all. There was no way I could explain to any of them what I just puzzled together.

All too soon, the sun lowered in the sky and our day at the beach drew to a close. I could sense the tension cresting between Lucas and Eli. I could feel the eminent death of their friendship like a fresh corpse. My heart and my mind were at war while I took in the strained feeling of our friendships. I was still trying to reconcile all that I knew about what the prophet was supposed to be, but I knew I needed to diffuse the current situation before it reached a climax that no one could walk away from.

Instead of switching places for the ride home, I opted to hop in the front seat of Eli's car, hoping to annihilate some of his frustration. Our day at the beach had started so well, yet ended so poorly, tainted by this indiscernible force. I could feel us all slipping through my grasp like the sand had earlier between my toes.

The ride home was silent and had slammed over all of us like two colliding cars. My mind raced with thoughts but none comprehensive enough to ease the visceral need to make this right. Forty-five minutes in the car and not one word was spoken. Evie and I sat staring out our own windows watching the passing cars, while Eli clenched and unclenched his hands on the steering wheel.

At one point, I turned to make a joke, but I saw the muscles in Eli's jaw ticking and heard Evie's almost inaudible sobs, so I opted instead to keep my mouth shut. I turned back to the window with a heaved sigh and rode the rest of the way home fighting my own unshed tears.

Eli pulled into my driveway just after dark; his car's headlights bounced off the garage door. No one moved but me. I hesitated with my hand on the handle of the car door,

but in the end, I didn't say anything as I grabbed my bag and
went inside.

CHAPTER SIXTEEN

I spent the rest of the weekend isolated in a dazed trance. I knew that I needed to confide in someone, but I didn't know who. I also had previously promised Evie that I'd help her prepare for the upcoming homecoming activities that weekend, but I couldn't wrap my brain around this new revelation and our freshly failing friendship dynamic.

It all seemed too raw and too fresh, like a rash from poison ivy that longed to be scratched. Everything had changed in that moment, and my world was spinning off kilter.

Sunday morning Mom had come by my room to see if I wanted to go to church with her like I always did, but I pretended to be asleep. She left me with a kiss on my forehead. By lunchtime, I had received a text from Lucas asking if I wanted to talk; but I ignored it as best as I could, too.

When Monday morning came, a pit of nerves had knotted and settled in my belly. I went through my morning routine with a hurried and disoriented feeling. I kissed my mom on the cheek, shutting the door behind me, and somehow made my way to the end of the driveway. Like clockwork, Eli and Evie pulled up.

Evie hopped out of the car with her usual bubbly personality, smiling as if nothing had happened. "You're going to have to ride in the back today. There are too many boxes in the back for my legs to fit."

I climbed into the car next to so much orange and black it looked like Halloween had puked all in the back of Eli's car. I shoved posters, banners, and streamers out of my way laughing at the overabundance of décor Evie had dreamed up. "Were you up all weekend making these?" I giggled as I shoved at a random balloon. Eli met my gaze in the rearview mirror with a furious look in his eyes. Evie just laughed as I now swatted a swarm of balloons out of my face.

Eli and I helped Evie hang all her premade decorations around the school before going about our usual class schedule. It had only taken most of first period, which was crazy considering how much she had hand made. By the time we made it to fourth period, I was beginning to feel a bit more normal, as if maybe Saturday hadn't been as bad as it had felt.

Eli barely made it into class before the bell rang. I expected him to take his usual seat by me, but he didn't. Instead, he sat in the front of the classroom by the door. The knot of fear that had eased returned in full force.

When the bell rang signaling lunch, Eli was the first out the door. I walked to the cafeteria alone, the pit of uneasiness building with each step I took. When I had made it into the cafeteria for lunch, I decided I wasn't hungry after all and made a beeline for the library instead. When it was finally time for the homecoming pep rally, I sat in my pre-appointed seat in the bleachers.

Evie gave a speech about community and togetherness. The whole time, I couldn't take my eyes off where Evie had the varsity football players sit. Eli found me the instant he sat down. I smiled and gave a little wave with my hand, but he just shook his head and proceeded to glare at Lucas for the remainder of Evie's speech, ignoring me completely.

Evie had lined all the varsity football players up in the middle of the gym floor. The cheerleaders danced their routine to the fight song in front of them. When the song ended, they sat with the football players. Abby took a seat beside Eli.

She smiled, flipped her long blonde ponytail, and flirted with Eli the entire time. He still wouldn't look at me. He knew where I was, but he was so focused on Abby and her beautiful smile that I seemed to melt into the mass of people in front of him.

The spectacle they were making ripped the breath right out of my lungs and tore my heart right out of my chest. I fought back sobs, ignoring the need to cry. I was angry and heartbroken, a sour combination that set my nerves aflame.

So, I turned to look at Lucas. He met my eyes with a pained expression before looking back to glare daggers at Eli and Abby. She giggled and playfully slapped Eli's arm, which in turn caused him to laugh, completely lost in their own world and oblivious to the speech his sister was making.

When the pep rally ended, I gathered my backpack and ran down the bleacher stairs out through the emergency exit as fast as I could before I lost it completely. Scalding teardrops slowly leaked from my eyes by the time I made it home.

Lucas had made it there before me, beating me with his truck by quite some time. He leapt from the truck, slammed the door shut, and didn't say anything as he grabbed me and pulled me to him. He held me as I tried to reassure him, I was okay. He finally seemed to believe me when he handed me a box of tissues.

I blew my nose and looked up at him still holding me solid in his large arms. "I'm sorry..." I sniffled "... I'm angry and my heart hurts in here, but it's bigger than that." I shook my head and gestured to my face. "I seem to be talking in circles a lot lately. I hate it."

He grimaced at my strained face. "Grace, you know you can tell me anything, right?" he asked hesitantly. I just nodded my head yes and tried to let it go. I refused to let the tears spill over that were threatening once again.

He took me by the shoulders, turning me to look up at him. "I'm begging, Grace, and you know that I don't beg. What is going on with you and Eli? And what happened Saturday?"

I sniffled before pulling out of his grasp. My mind whirled. How could I tell him? Finally, I just blurted it out before I could keep the words inside my mouth. "Evie is the prophet."

I let out a poof of air. His eyes grew round as saucers, his expression grew slack, and he made a little huffed whistling noise as if I had just sucker-punched him. Then he began to pace back and forth talking to himself, before finally collecting himself and turning back to me. "Are you sure?"

I nodded my head yes and replied, "I'm pretty sure." His mouth moved like a fish. "How?"

He looked away again and shoved a hand through his messy blonde hair. "How was the prophet this close the whole time and we didn't know? How did you piece it together?" He began pacing again.

"She umm..." I faltered, "... she had a piece of paper in her backpack that read sort of like a poem." He stopped pacing, sat down in the recliner next to the couch, and hung his head in his hands.

I tried to collect my thoughts, but they were just too scattered. "I wouldn't have thought anything about that paper being strange, except that it shocked me, not in the oh-my-gosh kind of way, but in the ouch-I-just-stuck-my-finger-in-a-light-socket kind of way." I rambled. "And if that wasn't already alarming, what was written on it was worse. I had this dream before we left for GUESS." I took a deep breath and let it out. "The poem was chanted repeatedly during that dream. I'd know that poem anywhere."

He stood and began pacing again. "We have to tell her."

I met his gaze. "I know, but I just don't know how."

We both jumped when we heard a jiggle on the front doorknob. Mom was home for the first night in a long while. With a quick wave of her hand, she said hello and went to make dinner. Over dinner, I recanted the entire tale to her, from the time I left for GUESS until that day's events, at which point, I started hiccupping sobs again. She held me until my sobs became sniffles and then stopped all together, murmuring comforting words while she gently stroked my hair.

Lucas left at some point during my tale, so I excused myself to the restroom and splashed cold water on my face before I returned to help her clean up the dishes. Completely exhausted, I trudged up the stairs and fell into a deep, dreamless sleep.

The rest of the week was the same, well aside from the tears. I refused to acknowledge the heartache in my chest. I didn't want it having wiggle room to make me go all sobbing and panicky. I had been a wreck too much lately.

I decided to change that, even though Eli wouldn't so much as look at me and opted to sit at the front of class. Abby sat next to him and fawned all over him during classes, between classes, and at lunch. I didn't eat lunch at all that week; I couldn't stomach sitting at that table.

Instead, I found myself alone under a large oak tree just outside the cafeteria. Ever since our school had consolidated four cafeterias into one large room, I found myself seeking the comfort of solitude. On the days when all my friends were busy, or I was just feeling the call of solidarity, I would sit in the shade and enjoy my lunch break observing the passersby. It was a beautiful, warm fall afternoon, but I didn't find myself enjoying the weather. I heard some sort of loud bantering and laughing coming from behind me, just on the other side of the tree.

I had been coming to this spot since my freshman year for one reason only—its isolation which, allowed me to withdraw and find confinement from the likelihood of dealing with bullies like Trent Jacobson, or T.J, as most called him.

Some kids said it meant total jerk, and I could see why. He and his group of depraved miscreants were picking on a special-needs kid who was part of a group visiting from a local junior high.

They had taken his sack lunch away and were tossing it around in a keep away fashion. They kept telling him to fetch like he was a dog. All the while, T.J. was throwing acorns from the oak tree at his back and making the defenseless boy squeal. I'd had enough of bullies like T.J. and Abby. I stood up from my spot and rounded the corner determined to teach the terrorists a lesson.

"Hey, you stupid meanie head," I shouted as I made my presence known. "Leave him alone, you snot bubbles". They had all stopped like they didn't understand why I was talking or what I was saying.

"She looks like a demented pixie," T.J. said. I walked over to bully number one and kicked him in the shin as I snatched the poor boy's glasses back out of his grasp.

The next timidly handed me the kid's lunch, and T.J. stood there looking at me as if I were a giant monster about to eat him. At this point, I wished I were.

I picked up a hand full of acorns and shot them one by one at T.J., giving him a taste of his own medicine.

I turned to the tormented boy and noticed Eli covering his mouth with a laugh, hiccupping "Meanie Head". His laughter bubbled over "Snot bubbles". He was gasping for air as he continued to shake with his uncontrollable laughter.

Apparently, he'd heard my temperamental explosion. Lucas was just standing there and staring at me wide eyed. I guess he, too, thought I looked like a demented pixie.

I ignored them both as I began to straighten the boy up. His glasses sat on his wide nose a little crookedly. I helped him brush himself off and made sure he didn't have any welts from the acorn assault. He seemed okay, a little traumatized but okay, none the less. I escorted him back to his group and told the teacher what had happened to the innocent kid.

The rest of my week, I sat at the tree alone. I felt as if I had no one to talk to. Nothing made sense. Aside from the brief acknowledgement of me the other day, Eli had completely ignored me. Lucas sometimes came outside to make sure I was okay. The rest didn't even notice my absence, which made my heart sink heavily.

By Thursday, Evie walked home with me. At least she was the one constant in my life. It had become our tradition to spend the night before the homecoming game prepping for that day's school spirit festivities.

CHAPTER SEVENTEEN

Football was a big deal in South Texas. Every fall during football season, football fields lit up in glorious displays. Once a season, there was a huge game that we called homecoming. Homecoming was the first game at the home stadium after a series of out-of-town games. Thousands of people flocked to the stadium for that game every year. Students, parents, football fans, former students, and faculty members got hyped up for the big game.

We wore a sort of corsage made of mums with ribbons and school spirit items dangling off them. Bells tinkled and jingled with every movement. Some were enormous, with multiple mum flowers; and some were small, with miniature mum flowers.

Through the years, many no longer had school colors in their corsages but opted for hot pink and blue zebra print, or rainbow colors. It was a personal preference. But we still wore school spirit colors in shirts, ribbons for our hair, face painting, etc.

We even had a specialty election, sort of like senior prom king and queen, except for homecoming, it was open to all class members. We elected those special members of court to reign over the festivities that year. There was the freshman class's lord and lady, the sophomore class's duke and duchess, the junior class's prince and princess, and, of course, the senior class's king and queen.

They were nominated by the student body for their contributions to the school and community. But let's face it, it was really just a popularity contest. The student body would then vote for the people they wanted to win.

The winner was usually announced during the homecoming game. We would end the week with a dance on Saturday. The dance was once held on Friday after the football game, but it left little time for us to enjoy the party, since there was a curfew and we girls had no time to primp after spending hours outside in the humid evening air watching the game.

Evie sidled up to me pulling a black t-shirt out of her bag. Look what I made you. The t-shirt had our mascot on the front, a burnt-orange yellow jacket, except the vinyl Evie used made him sparkle in the light. He looked fighting mad, as he usually did, and across the top, she put our school's name in big, shiny, metallic silver; and under the mascot, she put "Yellow Jacket Fan Club". I didn't turn the t-shirt around, but I could tell she bedazzled something on the back by the way the rhinestones pricked at my fingers.

We stayed up hours making our mums with the items we'd previously purchased. We put stickers on the ribbons to support our favorite two football stars and the year. We used traditional orange and black colored ribbons and white mums that year.

Some girls liked their mums to be huge and bright vivid colors. We'd even seen some the year before that were made of six large mums and were so big the girls had to use a braided cord to hold them around their necks. The poor girls tripped over the hundreds of long trailing ribbons that drug the ground.

Evie and I made ours the traditional size, one mum flower and only mid-thigh in ribbon length with a safety pin to fasten it to our shirt. After all, they did get heavy by the end of the day and no boys had bought ours to express their undying love for us. No, ours were made identically to express our support of our favorite team and players. Before finally dozing off to sleep, Evie got a bright idea and painted our nails alternating orange and black.

When we woke up to the sun shining through the curtains in the room, we were exhausted. Evie and I took turns plaiting two French braids in each other's hair and tying ribbons of orange and black in them. Then she painted numbers ten and twenty-two on each of my cheekbones. I did the same for her before we raced down the stairs to grab our backpacks. Mom met us at the door, camera in hand ready to snap a few pictures of us.

"Oh, girls, you outdid yourselves this year." She looked at each of our shirts and mums, trailing a finger over the delicate, dangling ribbons, then held up the camera and clicked a few pictures for us. Evie handed her phone over for a picture before we headed off for the day. "Have fun at the game today, you two. Tell the boys good luck for me," she said, as she kissed Evie's and my cheeks.

Eli was already there when we opened the door. He was leaning on the driver's side door and looked good enough to eat in his football jersey and blue jeans, arms crossed at his chest watching an ant crawl across the concrete.

He sucked in a sharp breath when he looked up and saw me, as if he hadn't had a good breath of air in a long time. He reached out and stopped me from making my way around him to put my bags in the back and climb in.

Evie rolled her eyes and stuck out her tongue at him behind his back before snatching my backpack from me and climbing into the backseat of the car.

"Grace," Eli whispered hoarsely as he pulled me around to face him. He reached up to run his fingers along the number ten on my cheek. His number. His lucky number. The same number I'd always worn in support of him since he'd played pee-wee football.

Aside from the prior year, when Abby decked herself out in all number ten paraphernalia she could manage while still wearing her cheerleader uniform. I couldn't stomach it, so I opted for just the painted cheek and the number hidden in my mum.

That year, though, in orange rhinestones Evie had bedazzled "E. Cole" across my shoulders and a large number ten that took up the entire rest of the back of my t-shirt when it was tucked in, exactly like the back and front of his football jersey.

He grimaced and looked me in the eyes, confusion written plain as day on his face. "Why?"

I flinched. His question felt like a punch to my heart. "Why not?" I stammered and shrugged my shoulders unable to meet his eyes. I glanced at Evie in the running car. She was busy typing something out on her phone, probably posting the picture of us on all her social media sites. I tried to pull away from Eli, but he didn't let me.

"It suits you," he said before he let me go. A cold shiver worked its way up my body from where his warm hand had touched my skin.

Puzzled as to what he was trying to say, I stepped away and moved toward the passenger side of the car. "What?" I asked baffled.

His eyes grew hungry like a lion looking at a gazelle. "My number. It suits you. Right where it belongs," he said fact like, before he visibly relaxed and slid into the driver's seat.

Confusion wracked through me, but I slid into the front passenger seat anyway. The entire ride to school, I couldn't get a handle on my emotions as they bounced and ricocheted inside my heart and my head. I couldn't place why it mattered so much to him that I wore his number that day. It was not the first time.

But, honestly, when I had finally seen the name and number on the back of my shirt, I absolutely refused to wear it. It felt wrong—as if he wouldn't have wanted me to have it. Evie was wearing Lucas's name and number and I told her we should just trade, but she insisted we were all friends and I was just being silly. So reluctantly, I took the shirt and put it on thinking maybe she was right. But then again, maybe she was wrong.

I tried hard to shake off Eli's contrasting behavior those last few weeks. I didn't know what it meant for fourth period and lunch, or what it meant between him and Abby; and I didn't understand why he pulled away so hard after insisting he liked me just on the Friday before when we were on our date. Oh my gosh! Was that only a week ago?

That hot and cold temperament of his was for the birds. Eli owed me a huge explanation, but I wouldn't press him for that, because, in honesty, maybe I owed him one, as well.

The day went like normal, though in the classrooms it was apparent even the teachers were relaxed and excited for our game that night, meaning we had loads of free time. I checked my phone periodically throughout the day.

Evie had indeed posted our picture on social media. Our smiling faces shined up at me with our arms around each other. Eli had shared it as well with the caption "My girls". My heart did a summersault at that. He had thirty-four likes on it so far and one mad frown. He'd also been tagged in several other pictures, including a few with Evie, Lucas, and, of course, one with Abby. I saved the picture to my phone.

I made it to class with Eli, still dreading that tension between us. But it appeared I had worried for nothing, because Eli was already sitting at our table. Eli motioned for me to come sit, so I did.

The bells on my mum jingled all the way. I had just finished plopping my backpack on the floor when he wrapped one of his big arms around me and said, "Smile!" I had just enough time to look up and smile for his selfie picture. Lucas joined in and photo bombed just in time. Eli did another without the Lucas photo bomb and ended up posting both anyway. I saved them, too. The room was loud with everyone's chatting.

Before long, we were off to lunch. I sat with the usual group but still wasn't hungry. The one-eighty flip in Eli had me so twisted and confused. It was like when his focus was with us, I lit up like the sun, bright and warm. But when he was brooding, it felt as if I were covered in thunder clouds, turbulent and rocky.

I opted to sit next to Evie, which left Eli the spot directly in front of me. That may not have been the best idea. He was like a magnet I couldn't draw my eyes away from. Any time I looked up, I met his smoldering gaze and would quickly look back down, or away at something else. Someone from the yearbook committee came by and snapped a few pictures of our table for the homecoming week foldout spread.

It was great with the five of us sitting together at lunch, especially on the day of the big game. We were all close friends and had been for many years, but it just seemed we had all kind of drifted these last few weeks.

It was a busy time at school with Eli and Lucas in football, Evie always immersed in some sort of school function, and Oliver, the jokester, constantly singing or performing on stage. Everyone had something keeping them busy. Everyone but me. Sometimes I seemed to be the glue that held us all together.

Something flew toward me, snapping me out of my own head momentarily. "Really Oliver?" I jeered at him teasingly. He thought it might be a good idea to start a small land war among us five, by launching the first attack—at me, no less, and with a stale french-fry right in my hair.

The others laughed as Eli took pity on me and flicked the fry off one of my braids. We each took turns tossing our own fodder at one another. It had been too long since the five of us laughed so hard.

Leave it to Oliver to try and steal the show by creating a snack catapult from plastic spoons and sending a grape halfway across the cafeteria. It suddenly went deathly silent. The silence was broken by Oliver sliding his chair back and screeching it along the tiled floor. "Time to go," he snickered.

We escaped just as the first retaliating launch of mashed potatoes was flung through the air to land with a splat on the window.

When lunch ended, Eli gently grabbed my arm. "Hey, can I talk to you a minute?"

I nodded my head yes, and said, "Of course, what do you need?" He seemed to pause, idly rubbing his bottom lip. He took a breath and was about to tell me what was on his mind, when shouting erupted in the hall.

A young teacher's aide ran down the hall and disappeared around the corner. I only had a moment to wonder who he was before a shrill screeching noise blasted us overhead.

I felt the room go still—the kind of stillness that only happens when something horrible is about to happen. Everything stopped—the strobing overhead light, Eli in mid-step reaching for me, the doors to the cafeteria. One by one, the lights in the hall exploded, sending shards of halogen bulbs raining in their wake.

The encroaching darkness enveloped even the sun shining through the windows with its inky blackness. Tendrils of smoke reached for Eli, but before they could touch him, my pendant wrapped itself around my hand to form my sword. It flashed something akin to a camera flash, blinding in its brilliance; but I had no camera in hand. The tendrils of darkness receded at the bright light, seeming to send it back wherever it had come from and sending time reeling forward.

Eli continued ushering me out the door, since that was protocol for fire drills. We met under the tree just outside the courtyard. It seemed no one knew what had happened. Only Lucas and I, that is. He gave me a pointed look that said, "We need to talk," without saying words. I was relieved to see Evie safely tucked into the shade of the huge oak tree.

By the time the fire department came and cleared the building, we had only one class left for the day. I didn't get a chance to speak with Lucas before he had to leave and prepare for the game. When school was finished, Eli and Lucas headed to the locker room, while Evie and I went home for a quick freshen up.

CHAPTER EIGHTEEN

We made it back just before the mad rush to get into the stadium. "Oh my gosh! I haven't seen this many people here in years," Evie gushed. "I'm glad they're all here to witness tonight; it's going to be epic. We're finally going to win," she squealed.

I just shrugged in disbelief. We never win our homecoming game, and rarely is it this packed at any game. At the rate of people flowing into the ticket booth, our stadium would hit maximum capacity, even though there was a slight chance it would rain.

Honestly, if it weren't for the fact that two of my friends were playing, I wouldn't have been there either. Football wasn't my thing. Sitting on an uncomfortable bleacher bench while watching sweaty, beefy guys throwing an odd-shaped ball back and forth, then chasing each other and knocking the other team's players down, only to dog-pile on top of them, while it was hot and humid in early October, wasn't exactly appealing to me. No, thanks. I'd take a comfy chair, a good book, a fuzzy blanket, and Lucky in my lap any day. But then again, I'd do anything for my friends, which was how I ended up there to begin with.

We wove our way through bag check and up to the stadium seating. Evie and I usually sat on the fifty-yard line, in the front-row seats. That way Eli and Lucas could always find us quickly. We saw Eli and Lucas tossing the ball back and forth in front of the track that ran around the new AstroTurf field.

Rumor had it that the school district had to replace the old grass field after some kid in a large truck drove onto the field and spun donuts in the middle of the fifty-yard line.

Eli and Lucas both stopped and waived when they saw us, breaking stride for only a moment. Before long, the referees called the coin toss in the visitor's favor. The marching band marched in to the cadence of the drums while the drill team marched in two by two to fill their seats.

The cheerleaders stretched and warmed up on the track. Abby sneered as she looked up in the bleachers then turned and called to Eli. Her perfectly coifed ponytail swung as she ran over toward him and threw her arms around him in one of those romantic kind of ways, except he gently shoved her off him and looked toward me in the stands. However, before he could tell her to let him be, the coach saw and shooed her away. I might have let out an unlady-like cackling laugh that ended with a snort.

Evie elbowed me in the side. "Ouch," I yelped as I grabbed my ribs.

"Let's go to the restroom before the game starts." Evie turned and began asking the couple next to us if they would save our seats. I looked at the clock. We only had ten minutes until kickoff. We would never make it back in time.

"Evie, I told you that we should have gone before we sat down. We won't make it back now."

Evie's mum jingled as she flailed wildly. "I didn't have to go then." She huffed as she stood and pulled me to my feet. We bumped and shoved our way against the flow of traffic going up the stairs only to stop just beyond the ramp. The line for the bathroom was extensive. I silently hoped the elderly couple next to us would save our seats.

The announcer started announcing the varsity cheerleaders that was followed with accolades. Of course, Abby received the loudest fan cheers. I glanced at Evie as she rolled her eyes and then started laughing. The announcer then went on to the good sportsmanship exchange and the rules and regulations.

We had just made it to the restroom doors when they held the moment of silence and the JROTC raised the flag to the varsity choir's rendition of the National Anthem. I hurriedly unpinned Evie's mum and held it. "Hurry," I mouthed as she brushed past people exiting.

She practically bowled over the next in line when she barreled back out. We moved to the side of the door, out of the waiting crowd's way, as I rushed to re-pin her mum.

"Don't you dare stick me with that, Grace," she exclaimed, as she noticed my shaking and hurried hands.

A loud burst of cheers erupted from the stands. "Ouch!" I'd jumped at the sudden burst of sound and jabbed the pointy needle into my finger. I hurriedly clasped her safety pin and popped my finger into my mouth to stop the bleeding.

"Oh shoot, they started without us." Evie gave a little pouty look, grabbed for my other hand, and pulled me along back up the ramp and to our seats in record time. Meanwhile, I flew along with her for the ride and sighed.

"I knew we'd miss the start of the game. What did we miss?" Evie asked the couple, who, thankfully, saved our seats.

"That number ten sure is a fast one," the elderly man excitedly recapped. "He caught the ball on the kickoff and ran it all the way for a touchdown only mere seconds after the game started. He was dodging people coming at him from every angle."

Evie squealed and clapped her hands. "That's my brother!" she proudly exclaimed.

I bounced my feet as I watched the game. The second play resulted in a flag thrown on the play. A player for the other team shoved one our players; and when he retaliated, that player grabbed his face mask and shoved him to the ground. We gained our first down due to the penalty.

The rest of the quarter, I sat and continued bouncing my knees and fidgeting with whatever I could get my hands on. The other team repeatedly fouled our boys and wouldn't let us gain any ground.

We went into the second quarter leading by one point, but that quickly changed. Halfway through the second quarter, Lucas, our quarterback, chucked the ball to Eli, the wide receiver. Eli took off running down the sideline and made a quick sharp turn toward the center of the field. Lucas had overthrown the ball, so Eli had to jump to catch it.

Evie and I both stood up and held our collective breaths while we watched in horror as Eli was blindsided in midair by the other team's tackle. Eli's helmet flew off on impact, and he landed with a sickening thud. It began to rain at that precise moment.

Evie's eyes glistened in the light, but I couldn't form comforting words to say to her. It was as if the entire planet took a breath and held it.

Rain pelted my face as I closed my eyes to shield myself from the sight of Eli splayed out on the field, but the scene continued to replay over and over in my head anyway. The crowd rose to their feet and a hush fell over them.

Minutes passed that felt like hours. My eyes flew open with the sudden burst of cheers and applause that echoed and bounced around the stadium as Eli limped off the field with the help of the athletic directors. Evie fell back into her seat, uselessly wiping under her eyes.

I hesitated a moment longer, trying to convince myself he was truly okay. He was laid out on the bench while he was checked over by EMTs and the team's trainers carrying boxes that closely resembled a toolbox. I tried unsuccessfully to see beyond the swarm of people around him.

Finally, he was pulled up into a sitting position, and, one by one, the crowd trickled away from him. When he was alone at last, he turned to us and waved. My heart tripled its beat.

The rain slackened to a mist as I raised my hand to wave in reply and decisively relaxed back into my seat.

As the time ran out on the clock for this quarter, the opposing team had scored another touchdown, causing them to be in the lead as we headed into halftime.

The rain had stopped, leaving us soggy and wet with ruined and rumpled mums. We watched Lucas run over to Eli, giving him a hand up and helping him hobble off with the rest of the team who were all running to the locker rooms. I was already ready for this game to end.

Usually, the halftime performances by the marching bands were my favorite part; but due to homecoming and the rain, they would be cut short. We watched the marching bands march in their intricate patterns. Pink and blue flags were tossed about while dainty dancers twirled them.

The baton twirler lit her batons on fire for the performance. It was the only time she would twirl them that season. Twirling fire batons was a school tradition during homecoming. Our school also lit up a giant letter "A" in flames, while the volunteer fire department stood ready to put out any residual fire. It was spectacular.

The homecoming court was crowned to applause. Then they were escorted off the field into waiting convertibles to ride once around the field waving like pageant winners. Abby was not crowned a winner, and I couldn't help but let a bit of happiness seep into my thoughts about that. I was not a jealous kind of girl, which was why I didn't express my thoughts out loud. I just really didn't like Abby. It was a mutual feeling, I'm sure.

Before long, the cheerleaders held up the banner as our guys ran through the paper and ripped it in half while the school song played, signaling halftime was over.

During the third quarter, the band and the varsity cheerleaders took a break. It was an oddly quiet quarter in the stands, too. There wasn't much to cheer about and not many people talked as they watched the game. In the end, we could only hold them at bay.

Eli was still benched when they signaled the start of the fourth quarter. He paced the sideline back and forth yelling and cheering for his teammates, following the same tracks the coach made. The opposing team scored another touchdown, which meant they were now leading the score by seven points.

The rain suddenly burst through the sky pelting us harder than the first shower. Eli was standing with his hands on his hips and his head hung while the rain soaked his hair. Stinging drops of rain slapped at my skin.

People ran out of the stands and down to the covered concession area. Only the most dedicated sat and watched the remainder of the game while the rain pinched and burned as it struck down on us.

We spent most of the last quarter trying to hold them off. They continually intercepted and kept us from advancing. The two-minute warning bell buzzed as the opposing team kicked the ball to our team, but we received the ball in our own end zone, an unusual play to say the least. The ball was brought out to the twenty-yard line as they set up again.

"Come on guys, we need this win!" Evie cheered. Lucas tried three different plays to get the ball down the field for our first down, but the ball still sat on the same twenty-yard line. Lucas called for a timeout and ran to the sideline to speak with the coach.

The coach motioned for one of the guys to run off the field. He sloshed muddy water as he ran. Their burnt-orange and black uniforms now clung to them, lifeless, outlining every indention in the pad they wore. The referee blew to signal the end of the timeout.

Lucas turned wide eyes to me as he and Eli ran back on the field with fifty-four seconds on the clock. The crowd was on its feet yelling and cheering instantly, but the rain steadily poured. Eli flung his wet hair back and poured out the water that was collecting inside his helmet before strapping it back on.

Evie and I were standing and holding on to each other waiting to see the outcome. We both knew Eli was playing injured and were praying he'd stay safe. They would need a miracle to pull off a win, but we all held on to the last shreds of hope.

The guys lined up, as the seconds ticked by. The ball was snapped to Lucas. Eli and two other players took off running as fast and as far as they could, while Lucas slipped on the AstroTurf as he dodged the other team's attempts to tackle him. During his attempt to dodge them, he dropped back to the ten-yard line, an entire thirty feet in the opposite direction we needed the ball to move.

The old man next to us exclaimed in disbelief, "There is no way he can make it!"

Evie looked to me and shrugged her shoulders. I knew, if anyone could, Lucas could make the throw. After all, he was playing with an advantage the others didn't have. Eli split off from the other two players at the fifty-yard line and ran to the corner.

The old man once again asked in disbelief, "What on earth is that boy doing now?" Eli had just passed the twenty-yard line when Lucas threw the ball to him.

Eli dove for the ball, as he rolled into the end zone. Time went stationary for me. Rain stood frozen, as sheets of water droplets stood between Eli, Lucas, and me. They were like the sun and the moon working in tangent when they were on the field together. Eli's touchdown had put us one point away from tying the game.

I watched in slow motion, as they set up again on the three-yard line, trying hard to will it back into normal time. My heart picked up its pace as if it lived outside of my body. The entire stadium went silent; some stood in mid cheers. My heart thump-thumped twice. Hard. I reached to touch my chest; I thought I was having a heart attack. Thump, thump. It slammed again into my ribcage trying to free itself from its prison of bone.

There were only three agonizing seconds left on the clock. Rain trickled slowly in their stalled state. I blinked once the ball was hiked to Lucas. My breathing intensified and grew ragged. I couldn't focus on anything but inhaling and exhaling.

Lucas began to glow like that of Raguel, the only other angel I had seen. He immediately handed the ball off to Eli. I blinked again and looked at Evie as my heart made another attempt to flee its prison. She too was lit up with an erethreal halo of light. I looked back toward Eli as a bright burst of silver light hit my eyes.

My heart ceased. My breath stopped. I froze.

I watched in slow motion unable to do anything else. Eli took only one step forward before he jumped six feet into the air over the top of the other team's lineman landing with a detonative shock wave that sent rain and mud flying into the air in his wake.

The rain rippled outward from the sound waves clearing the space between him and me as if it were raining all around us and we were under a bubble of protection. The wave of raindrops splashed me in the face, sending time spiraling forward as he landed in the end zone to score again.

I sucked in a huge breath of air. The crowd erupted in cheers. We had won. The guys picked up Eli and carried him off the field toward the locker room. His eyes met mine. He quirked his lips up in a grin and winked from his perch on the team's shoulders, as they disappeared into the locker rooms.

He knew. He knew what he was, and he knew that I now knew as well.

Evie elbowed me in the side and popped a bubble in her gum. "Told ya we'd win, and it was going to be epic." She winked.

I still stood dumbfounded for what seemed like only seconds but in reality, was likely twenty minutes. I jumped when Evie touched my shoulder.

"You ready to go?" Her eyebrows rose with the question.

Breathlessly, I said, "Yes." She linked her arm in mine and marched us down to wait at the locker room doors.

Traditionally, we would head over to Sonic for a snack after the game. That night, however, I needed to escape but couldn't see my way out.

Eli and Lucas came out the door as I paced back and forth splashing mud all over my shoes and up my legs. I was panting as if I couldn't get enough air. Eli looked at me and ran back inside for a towel.

He returned and grabbed my hand to pull me along behind him. He found a small ledge by the side of the fencing that ran around the stadium and sat me down. I stared at him, unable to form words and feelings. Evie and Lucas shuffled up beside us.

"Is she okay?" Lucas asked

Was I okay? I didn't know anymore. I felt like a hollow shell of a human. I knew that I should have been feeling something; instead, this strange calm wound its way into my body and settled in. I just needed to remember to breathe.

Eli handed me the towel. I registered that it smelled like him and that it was a soft beige color. I sat there cradling it as if it were a living thing. His eyes sparkled in the moonlight. The lights made his skin seem to glow a slivery blue color. He looked alien. He laughed as I held the towel, unsure what to do with it. His irises began to swirl a molten metallic silver and glow in the semi-darkened lights.

I took a breath and let it out slowly, then proceeded to wipe the mud from my legs and shoes. I folded the towel as he grabbed my hand and pulled me along to his car.

Once I was positioned to his liking into his front seat and the towel discarded in the back, he started his car and pulled out of the player's parking lot. He fidgeted with the steering wheel for a few minutes before turning on the radio. I sat with my hands folded in my lap looking anywhere but at him.

We pulled up into the drive-through. He slammed the car into park and turned his body to face mine. I needed out of the car. My skin was crawling as if ants were marching all over me. I couldn't get enough air into my lungs. I reached for the door handle to get out, but he locked the car door. I slid against the door as far away from him as I could get.

"Grace." He whispered my name as if it were his prayer. "It's okay, Grace," he said. "I need to hear you tell me it's okay."

I shook my head. "I can't do that," I whispered breathlessly. My hands trembled. He reached across the armrest for one of my hands as if I were a feral kitten and would run away from him. He pulled me closer to him. I was suddenly overwhelmed by his cologne. He smelled like home. My home.

Shivers tormented my body. "Eli..." I pulled away. He put his finger to my mouth to stop me from talking.

He sighed and hung his head. "Not today, Grace, please. We just won our homecoming game. Don't wreck me today. Please. Just tell me it's okay," he pleaded.

I nodded as my heart was breaking. "It's okay," I relented.

It was anything but okay.

He smiled and unlocked the doors. He ran around the hood of his car and slid across to open my door. I let out a painful laugh.

He pulled me out of the car, picked me up in one of his bear hugs, and spun me around. "We won!" he shouted. I couldn't help the laugh that escaped as he twirled me around making me dizzy.

Evie and Lucas arrived, and I decided to lock my thoughts into a box and open it later alone. I put on my bravest and happiest expression and ate the celebratory ice cream sundae. I listened as they recapped the best and the worst moments of the game. They were all so vibrant and shining.

In that moment, I wanted to give up everything to keep them all safe. My necklace warmed against my skin in warning. I felt the darkness creeping in from the back corner of the building. I saw in clarity that it was about to disrupt this happy moment.

I excused myself as I walked toward the shadow. Lucas appeared by my elbow a moment later. "I felt it," I stated simply. He nodded in agreement.

My sword slid into place. I looked directly into the inky-black spot that was forming into a man. "I'm only going to state this once. Leave or die." I growled as I widened my stance, prepared to strike. Lucas was just behind me, out of my way but close enough to help if this came to a fight.

Echoing in a thousand whispers swarmed my ears. I struck out with my sword at the darkening blob.

I heard them say in unison, "They're ours, light bearer. Maybe not today, maybe not tomorrow." I felt the breath of one brush my ear. "But they will be ours."

I spun toward the breath of air and shouted, "Who are you?"

The voices replied in their whispered, diverse cadence, "We are many." A gust of wind tossed the ends of my hair. "We are legion." The voices cackled.

At once, the darkness that had been forming dispersed.

I stood staring into the dark until my sword was safely around my neck and the light blinked on above the back entrance of the restaurant.

Lucas brushed my shoulder as he nodded for us to go back to the celebration.

I looked to the glittering twin lights laughing playfully with each other. The prophet and the law giver side by side.

CHAPTER NINETEEN

That night, sleep came fitfully, fighting and tugging. My mind buzzed. Finally, I caved into sleep. It was dark—the kind of darkness that could only be felt, the kind that spoke of an emptiness of light.

I was trembling from the cold so bitter my bones felt frail and brittle. "Not here again," I said through clenched teeth. I squeezed my eyes shut and willed myself out of the pit.

When I opened my eyes, I could feel the wind biting and tugging at my skirt, whipping my hair about. I could hear the clanking armor growing louder as it drew near. Standing at the edge of the cliff I willed myself to move yet again.

The Roman battle cries made my eyes fly open. Javelins pummeled horses and men alike. A chariot raced for me. I stood my ground and willed the scenery away.

I felt the weight of the chainmail settle over me as the wisps of the Roman battle faded into the mist and the battle cries of the crusades took their place. My opponent drew near. He was speaking, but no longer could I hear what was said. It was only he and I; the rest of the scene was poorly developed through the dense murky fog. "God," I called out, shoving this landscape and scene aside.

The room where I had met God previously took shape and instantly, I relaxed, feeling free of danger. I looked around, but he wasn't there. Disappointment flooded my heart as my eyes began to burn.

"God, I need you. Please tell me what I have to do," I pleaded as I broke down. My friends were in danger. I couldn't fail them. I needed his help. I sank to my knees as I hung my head in defeat, and my heart was ripped into.

"Please," I whispered. His comforting arms embraced me, and he began to soothe my tears. He held me silently in the misty room and let me cling to him as a child clings to his parent for comfort. He held me and cradled me to his chest. I looked up into his eyes, afraid of the answers I found there.

"I thought you wouldn't come." I shook my head and hung it in shame. "I thought you had left me alone when I needed you the most."

"You are never alone, Grace." He smoothed the wispy hair back from my face. "I am always here with you."

Deep down in my heart, I knew it was true; but with everything that was happening, I had never felt more isolated and alone. I was a lost ship in a turbulent ocean, and he was my only safe harbor.

"What do I do?" I whispered, afraid to really ask the question and more afraid of the answer I might receive.

He took me by the chin and lifted it, to look into his eyes. "You tell them the truth," he stated simply.

I shook and hung my head in disagreement. That answer seemed too easy and too complicated all at the same time.

He lifted my face up again to meet his eyes. "Grace, you called upon me. Have I not answered you in this secret place of thunder?" He gestured to the room.

I felt at once ashamed of my doubt. I nodded my head. "Yes, yes, you have."

His voice grew stern. "Then hear me now. Truth is the only answer I must give you. You have the tools you need to accomplish this task." He lifted his eyebrows as if trying to make me understand what he was saying.

I nodded my head suddenly in understanding. "The mirror," I said, with a sigh.

"Yes, the looking glass." His smile was brilliant, and he kissed my forehead. "I am so proud of you, my dear girl."

He patted my back before pulling away and pulling me to my feet. "You must hurry; this task cannot be put off any longer. The time is drawing near."

"Will I see you again?" I turned and asked with a squeak, but he was no longer there with me.

His voice boomed in reply, "When you call on me, I will answer you."

I awoke with the sun shining through my curtains and Lucky licking my chin. Evie had slept over to get ready for the homecoming dance. She wanted to go shopping at the mall, but I didn't know if that would be in the cards for us anymore.

I went to my dresser and picked up the antique hand mirror, then tiptoed silently to Evie's backpack, hoping she hadn't removed the poem from it. My fingers found it quickly when the paper shocked me again. I raced down the stairs with the treasures in hand to find Evie sitting at the table eating a bowl of Fruity O's.

"Good morning," she beamed.

"Good morning" I replied hastily. My heart began to thump at an abnormally fast rate, hammering its rhythm inside my chest.

Evie shoved the box of cereal at me. I picked it up and set it aside. Before I let my nervousness get the better of me, I needed to tell her.

"Evie, I need to tell you something, and I need you to promise me you won't freak out," I proclaimed a little too loudly. Evie's eyes grew round, and she opened her mouth as if she was going to speak. I waved her off. "Please don't; I need to say this before I lose my nerve," I said before she could interrupt me.

"Okay," she peeped and mime-zipped her mouth shut. I took a deep breath in and exhaled to compose myself before I continued. "So, I know you've noticed some strange things lately, especially where I am concerned." Her head bobbed yes.

"Well, there is a reason for that, one I am still trying to get used to." I cleared my throat and began to fidget with the mirror. "I am going to tell you a story first." Evie all but abandoned her breakfast.

"Three thousand years ago, before man, God created angels." She narrowed her eyes at me, but I continued.

"Lucifer was the most beloved angel; he was exceptionally beautiful and known. However, he grew angry at God." She rolled her eyes and huffed, growing more impatient with my tale.

"He was angry because he felt that God favored man more. He convinced a third of the angels in heaven to follow him and rebel against God. God stripped them of their heavenly rights and cast them out of heaven." I watched as she squinted her eyes at me, trying to see where I was going with my story.

"Lucifer and his fellow fallen angels created an army, Lucifer being the general. While chained in the Lake of Fire, his hubris grew exponentially vengeful. In heaven, amid these rebellious dissension in ranks, God sent the remaining angels down to earth to find warriors to fight for humanity with the holy angels." I fidgeted with my shirt, trying hard to express what I wanted to say to her.

"They made a pact called The Patriarchs' Covenant with the worthiest human beings on the planet—Elijah, the prophet, and Moses, the law giver." I shuffled the paper in my hand.

"The covenant stated that their descendants would carry out the burdens of being the prophet and the law giver until the end of time." I looked back at her; this time her face was pinched with confusion.

"The prophesy stated that the public execution of these two humans would bring about the end of the world." I cleared my throat and swallowed. "There have been many attempts on these beings' lives. Every generation of the prophet and law giver has been met with trials, hardships, and spiritual warfare, but never have the anointed ones been executed."

She crossed her arms and huffed. "Grace, you're being weird. Does this have to do with why you've been acting bizarre and why you're looking at me like I just ran over a cute little animal."

I shoved the paper over at her. "How did you know about that?" I asked, gesturing to the paper that now was in her hands.

"I don't know, Grace. I just see things sometimes. I don't know why, and I don't know how; it just happens."

I shook my head in agreement. "But I do know why." I slid the mirror toward her across the table. "Evie, you are the prophet, and Eli is the law giver."

"Oh, give me a break, Grace. That's super creepy. What have you been reading that would give you these ideas?" her voice growing louder with each word. I felt her denial as thick as smog looming in the air.

I gestured to the mirror. "If you don't believe me, look in the mirror and see for yourself. That mirror will show you the truth."

"Oh, so what you're going to tell me that God or some angel gave you this magic mirror and told you to show me?" She held the mirror in front of her and peered in at her reflection.

I don't know what she saw; but her face paled and sweat broke out on her forehead as tears welled in her eyes. She suddenly scraped the chair back across the floor and dropped the mirror on the ground as she ran outside.

"Evie!" I called after her. I stooped to pick up the mirror and continued my chase.

"Go away, Grace; don't talk to me ever again. I want no part of what ever crazy O's you've been eating," she screamed as she ran down the sidewalk toward her house.

She was causing a scene. Mr. Hathaway, the elderly widower next door, stopped to watch the escapades on his morning walk to retrieve the newspaper. "Mornin', Grace; it's a beautiful day out. Everything all right with you girls?"

I stopped and let Evie escape. After all, it's exactly what I had done when I learned the truth as well.

I turned back toward my own house. Mornin', Mr. Hathaway. Beautiful day. Everything's fine, sir; have a good day."

I rushed to close the front door and sank down in the couch. Lucky plopped his body up and into my lap. "It's going to be okay, right Lucky?" I asked as I gingerly patted his tummy while staring absently at the floral-patterned wallpaper in front of me. "It'll be okay." I repeated.

CHAPTER TWENTY

By noon, it was evident Evie wasn't coming back. She wouldn't answer her phone or any of my texts. So, I gathered her backpack, clothes, and things from my room and dropped them off with her mom, because Evie refused to come to the door.

I broke down and called Lucas. "Hey, can you come over?" I asked.

"Sure, what do you need?"

I sighed. "I'll tell you when you get here."

Fifteen minutes later, I answered the door to a flushed Lucas. "What's up?" he asked as he brushed past me into the living room.

"Where to start." I crossed my arms and collapsed into the recliner. "Eli is the law giver. I suppose you caught that last night."

"Yep." He nodded as he sighed.

"I told Evie," I blurted out and looked up into his face.

He raised his eyebrows and widened his eyes "You what?" he exclaimed.

I closed my eyes and sighed, "I told Evie; I even tried to show her the truth with the mirror. No, not mirror, looking glass," I said as I tossed it on the coffee table closer to Lucas.

He looked down at it and then reluctantly looked back up at me. I gestured for him to pick it up. When he did, his eyes grew round as saucers. He gasped and dropped it back onto the coffee table.

"Where did you get the looking glass?" He swallowed thickly, eyeing the mirror as if a monster were about to crawl out of it.

"You know, I didn't stop and ask God where he got it, when he handed it to me. I didn't even ask him what it does, being that I was shocked that I was even speaking with God." I picked up the mirror and held it in my hands.

Nothing happened when I peered into it. I just saw my own pale face with wide eyes that had darkened circles under them. I sighed and set it back on the table.

"What did you see in there?" I asked, surprised by his repulsion to the mirror.

"I..." he stammered. "I saw blood raining from the sky. I saw you and your sword. I saw Lucifer free." He closed his eyes, pinched the bridge of his nose, and shook his head as if to clear whatever vision he saw in there.

"Okay." I swallowed. "That brings me to point two. I have to go to the mall, and I'm pretty sure that Evie is going there too. We cannot leave Eli and Evie alone. I was told that the time is near, and I couldn't wait."

He seemed to understand where I was going with that thought. "That means whatever it is that's about to happen could happen at any time."

I nodded my head. "Exactly."

"Well, when I passed their house, I saw Eli and Evie climbing into his car. I guess we know now where they are headed." He stood and grabbed his keys out of his pocket and gestured for the door.

I gave Lucky a pat on the head and left him to chew his bone on the couch.

Lucas flew the thirty minutes to the mall, which was in construction. I was surprised he didn't kill us or, at least, get a ticket.

He threw the truck in park and turned to me before getting out of it. "Where are we headed?"

I glanced at my watch; it was almost lunch. "The food court." He nodded, and we raced as fast as we could to the food court.

I grabbed Lucas's arm to slow him down just as we entered and the smells of all the different restaurants hit our nostrils at once. Evie and Eli were in line for pizza, all the way across the court.

Lucas understood my hesitation at meeting up with them. Instead, he gestured for a safe distance away. "You find us a table there; I'll grab us something to eat. We can watch them from here without being conspicuous.

I nodded and took off for the general area he had indicated. Since it was a Saturday, the mall was slammed. The food court was overflowing with people. Tables were thrown together haphazardly to accommodate enough seating for large families with wheelchairs and strollers.

I found us a spot in between a couple on a date and a family with toddlers, who were slinging food all over as the mother tried to feed them small bites of chicken nuggets.

Evie and Eli were within eye sight, but we wouldn't be noticeable. Lucas arrived with our food and drinks.

I absentmindedly played with the fries on my tray and took small tentative bites of my hamburger as Lucas tried but failed to engage me with small talk. I was too preoccupied with the twins to notice his increasing frustration.

When they stood to leave, I stood too. Lucas grabbed our trays and threw our trash away before coming back and gesturing me to follow.

Evie was obviously in a shopping mood. She dragged Eli to every store imaginable. The poor guy looked tortured about three stores into the escapade. Lucas looked similarly tortured.

Finally, she stopped at a boutique dress shop. I wanted to go in and look, but the shop was one of the smaller ones at the mall. We'd have been way too noticeable. We opted to go into the soap shop next door, instead, so that we could keep an eye on the exit.

Lucas excused himself, it took about fifteen minutes before he made his way back into the soap shop carrying two sodas and a pretzel. I raised an eyebrow at his purchases.

He took a bite of his pretzel and shrugged his shoulders. "Shopping makes me hungry."

I burst out laughing at his admission. "Thank you for the soda." He nodded his head, as he shoved another bite into his mouth.

Evie left the shop with yet another bag, this time a long garment bag. I longed to see which dress she picked for herself. It made me a bit sad that I wouldn't know until tonight. I'd just hoped that she'd talk to me again.

We followed them all the way to the parking lot. I looked at my watch; it was close to time for us to get ready. I sighed. I wanted a new dress since I had already worn mine to the GUESS dance. Lucas started the engine and pulled onto the road. He glanced quickly at me. "What's wrong?" he asked.

"Nothing really. It's not important." I turned to peer out the window.

He gave me an incredulous look. "Come on, what's eating you, aside from the obvious?"

I sighed again and quietly stated, "I wanted a new dress since I've already worn mine." I shook my head to clear away the longing I was feeling. "But really, you were the only one who saw me in it from around here, and it's not like I have a date tonight like I had hoped."

He laughed and wagged his eye brows. "Oh, what a coincidence; I don't have a date either." He looked back at the road, "I liked that dress. You were radiant." I smiled and laughed a little at his obvious flirting.

Lucas dropped me off at home to get ready for the dance. "Hey, Grace. Pick you up at six tonight," he said as he put the truck into reverse.

"Hey", I turned around and walked back toward him, "I just thought of something. How are we going to watch them while we're primping for tonight?"

He smiled and winked. "Already on it," he replied, as he backed out of the driveway.

CHAPTER TWENTY-ONE

Mom met me just inside the door. "Hey, sweetie." she walked up and hugged me, still smelling like the alcohol-based antiseptic and bleach the hospital used. "Where is Evie?" she asked as she looked to the empty entry hall behind me. I shook my head. "Oh, sweetheart, I'm sorry; what happened?" she asked, as she tugged me into the living room.

"I told her the truth." I replied, as I flopped down into the couch next to Lucky, still busy with his bone.

Mom sucked in a stern breath. "Oh, I see." She sobered "Well, then we better hurry to get you ready to go."

Mom helped me to curl and pile half of my hair on top of my head with pins. She went through hundreds in her quest to tame the fine limp mess I had for hair. The rest of my hair hung in delicate ringlets down my back.

She expertly applied my makeup—light, gold-reflecting eyeshadow and highlighter, with just a hint of color to my cheeks and lips. I looked grown up.

"I have a surprise for you," she said as she walked to her closet. "I know you wanted a new dress, but how about a borrowed one instead?" She pulled out a deep navy-blue, short A-lined dress with a high-low skirt and off-the-shoulder gold sleeves. The dress was so dark it looked almost black.

As she held the dress to me, I could see the light reflect from a delicate, embroidered, pale-golden lace overlay. I had never seen this beautiful dress before, but it fit my mother's elegant style perfectly.

"I think this one will fit you." She looked at me and her smile fell. "You don't like it?" she glanced at the dress considering it a bit crestfallen as she stood and extended toward me.

"Oh, mom no. That's not it. It's beautiful. It's just that I have never seen you wear that dress before." I knew there was a story behind it. I realized that I should have gone exploring in my mother's closet before now.

She smiled, showing the tiny lines in the corner of her eyes. "It's from another lifetime." Her eyes took on that faraway look as if she were remembering a fond memory from a life I didn't know.

I didn't ask her about it. It seemed like a memory just for her. I reached to take the hanger and the dress from her, as she seemed to dismiss her lingering memories.

"Oh," she snapped her fingers and abruptly turned toward the closet again. "Shoes, I have shoes that match." She shuffled through several boxes at the top of her closet before she found the ones she wanted.

"Ah ha, here they are." She dusted the top of the box off and thrust it into my hands.

"Go on." She waived as she shooed me out of the room and into the adjoining master bathroom.

I glided into the dress, anticipating the evening to come. It was a bit tight in the waist but fit perfectly, otherwise. The off-the-shoulder sleeves of the dress were beaded in a swirling floral pattern.

I let my fingers trail along the softly adorned material covering the dress. I felt the silky fabric that circled around my waist where the bodice of the dress met the translucent golden panel overlaid on to the navy gown. I inspected my reflection in the mirror and twirled around watching as the skirt swished around my knees.

I swiftly opened the shoe box, sliding the tissue aside to reveal the matching strappy-sandaled heels that lay inside. They were a taller heel, which I was not used to wearing, but they were beautiful.

The buckled straps of the shoes were made of the same navy satin as the dress, but the part that went across the toes was a solid piece of adorned opaque fabric, which also matched the elegant overlay of the gown. It was obvious to me these were custom made to match the dress and must have cost a small fortune.

I was slipping into the last shoe when mom knocked at the bathroom door. "Come in," I called, absently fiddling with the buckle on the shoe. She opened the bathroom door and sucked in a deep breath. Tears glistened in her eyes as she looked me over.

"Oh, baby, you look so beautiful." She pulled me into a motherly embrace. She pulled away and lifted her hands as if in prayer. "Humm, this needs something," she stated before turning back into the bedroom. I followed close behind, wondering what, exactly, it was she would unknowingly reveal next.

She stopped at her dresser and opened her small jewelry box that had lain there unmoved and unopened for as long as I could remember. I smiled at my own memory about that box.

When I was five, I had seen it on one of our morning cuddle sessions in her room and had asked if I could play with her treasure box. She tickled my tummy and told me no, that inside of that pretty treasure box were her treasures and someday I would have my own.

I had pouted and begged but she just changed the subject. When she went downstairs to make us some breakfast, I had slipped back into her room quietly and grabbed the box of what I imagined were thousands of sparkling treasures and snuck back into my room as silently as I could, like a thief from the old cartoons.

As hard as I tried, I couldn't get the treasure box to open. I even had tried dropping it onto the floor to shatter like my dolly did when she fell from the shelf. I then tried to smash it with the door like I once had done to my fingers, which gave me a boo-boo for a week. The treasure box still refused to reveal its wondrous secrets.

Mom heard all the commotion and rushed into the room thinking I had hurt myself. Instead she found me with the box. My mom bent down to me and looked me in the eyes. She tenderly pried the secret box from my tiny hands. She then gently explained to me that what I had done was wrong and told me she was disappointed that I took something that wasn't mine. She told me not to touch it again. I told her I was "sowy" and that I just wanted to see the pretty treasures. She kissed my little chubby cheek and picked me up to carry me to breakfast.

Later that afternoon she took me to the store and bought me my own jewelry box and a few tiny treasures to hide inside.

My jewelry box still sat on my own dresser. It had a pink and gold unicorn carousel adorned on the scratched and dented white painted wood. Inside was a miniature ballerina that danced in front of a tiny mirror on a pastel-pink velvet stage. I could still hear the music that the jewelry box played.

"Here we go," Mom said as she turned to me and held up twin tiny diamond and gold drop earrings, abruptly snapping me out of my trance. I took them and gently hooked them into my ears.

I paused only a moment to notice that the rest of my mother's secret treasures were still safely locked away in her jewelry box. I smiled to myself and adjusted the last earring into place.

CHAPTER TWENTY-TWO

Lucas arrived moments later. I heard his noisy truck as it turned into our drive way. "Well, my ride is here." I softly spoke to my mom.

She nodded and gestured for the staircase. We made it downstairs just as he knocked. Mom picked up a small, silver, hand-held camera that sat on the entry table to the right of the door—the same camera she had been using for years, also, the same camera she had used to capture the last pictures of Evie and me just yesterday morning.

"May I please have a photograph of you both?" she hesitantly asked.

Lucas flashed his brilliant smile, his eyes alight enjoying my torture. "Oh, yes ma'am. Sure."

I rolled my eyes. "Mom, this isn't a date," I said as we moved into somewhat of a normal prom pose for the picture.

Mom, who was already focused on the settings of the camera, momentarily popped her head up to look at us. "Okay, honey, but I still want a picture." She moved back into position behind the automatic lens and snapped, what felt like, more than thirty pictures before she let us leave. I hugged her and thanked her again before I rushed out the door dragging Lucas lazily behind.

We made it to the gym in record time. We could hear the music thumping all the way at the back of the parking lot. Lucas took off at a fast pace, my legs struggled to keep up with his stride. I could see his shoulders wagging up and down as he trotted along.

When I had finally caught up with him, I looked toward him. He was continually fidgeting with his tie as we walked into the gym. I shook my head and silently laughed as I jumped to stand in front of him, abruptly halting his fast pace. He stumbled to a standstill, just in time.

His eyes widened with how close we were. He towered over me, even with my tall heels on. I gave him a soft close-lipped smile that didn't quite touch my eyes. He swallowed as I reached up and moved his hands out of my way, subsequently exposing his lopsided, silky, black necktie.

"We're late," he said a bit impatiently.

"I know," I said, as I looped the tie around the collar of his shirt.

"We need to go, Grace." He gestured to the building behind me.

I nodded again, widening my eyes expressively.

"I know, but you never can seem to get this tied correctly." I giggled as I worked the new knot up to the top button on his dress shirt, careful not to touch the black jacket of his tux.

When I finally had it settled into a normal place, we hurried the rest of the way to the gym.

Abbey was at the front entrance selling and taking pre-purchased tickets. Lucas pulled ours out of his jacket pocket and handed them over to her. She slid her pink manicured fingertips up his hand and traced tiny circles in his outstretched palm, instead of just taking our tickets.

My eyes threw daggers at her while she smiled and flirtatiously batted her eyes at Lucas, who, for all she knew, was my date. My necklace warmed at my growing anger. I knew I needed to relax. She tested every ounce of patience and calm I had when she opened her mouth and spoke.

"Hi, Lucas. Great play last night." She cooed as she swung her hair over her shoulder and bit her plump, pink bottom lip with her perfectly straight white teeth.

She wore her white-blonde hair curled and loose around her shoulders. Her hot-pink dress was tight and accentuated her curves.

"Save me a dance," she stated, her eyes dancing as she flirted.

"Thanks," he uttered, uninterested in whatever she was playing at and not responding to her dance request, much to her dismay. He then jerked his hand away from her and put the tickets on the table.

He turned to me and held out his arm while giving me one of his thousand-watt smiles. "Ready?" he asked, as if his eyes were only for me. I knew it was for show, but I admittedly liked the shade he threw at Abby and the attention he gave to me.

I smiled brightly as I took his elbow and we both turned to walk inside. I didn't miss the hurt that crossed Abby's face as he brushed her off and dismissed her.

It was then that I felt a small amount of empathy for her. "See you later, Abby," I called back, trying to soften the ego punch she had received from Lucas. She snorted as she crossed her arms and turned away from me.

Inside, it was packed with bodies; there wasn't much moving around room. The boom-boom from the speakers and the unmistakable gymnasium smell greeted us first as we passed the area where the refreshment table was set up. The line was full of people waiting already.

Next, it was orange, black, and white everywhere. The entrance of the gym had a floating balloon arch with a balloon image of our mascot hanging in the center.

Evie had covered the walls of the gym with black paper to darken the room. She had then hung streamers on the ceiling, looping in a spiral pattern from the center of the gym. It looked like a large orange, white, and black star had burst from the ceiling and continued its explosion down the walls.

She had even brought in a disco ball to hang in the middle, for the full exploding effect. Where the streamers ended, school-colored balloons were hung or left to float around the room, creating a moving wave as your eyes circled the area. To the right of the arch, was where I found Evie greeting everyone as they made their way in.

I made my way over toward her, but she overlooked me, choosing, instead, to greet Lucas. She made it seem as if I didn't even exist—similar to how Abby treated me most of the time. But when Evie ignored me, it felt as if she were jabbing a sword in to my chest.

She had chosen a light silvery grey high-low satin dress. It was sleeveless with a tight diamond-studded bodice, then flared into a flowing A-line skirt. She wore silver accented earrings and a tiny diamond pendant around her neck. Her dark hair was put into a beautiful chignon bun. She was stunning. Then again, she always was.

Lucas tugged me reluctantly to the dance floor. We swayed to the music as we scanned the room for threats. We danced, unaware of how long, and not really paying attention to each other—like robots piloting human bodies. Weirdly animated, disjointed, and disconnected from each other.

I noticed the tempo changed to an upbeat song. I looked up to Lucas about to pardon myself off the dance floor. It was then that I noticed the couple tucked away in the small corner opposite from us. My body instantly stilled.

I had involuntarily halted my sway to the music's rhythm and, instead, went rigid at the sight of Eli. My heart pounded inside my ribs. I felt each beat slam inside my chest. I would have sworn its pounding was visible outside of my torso, like the wolf from the old cartoons, complete with the eyes that bugged a foot out of his head.

Eli's black leather shoes shined with the twinkling of the disco ball. His suit fit him well, as if it were tailor-made just for him. My eyes traveled up to his broad shoulders. His satin tie was the same pale silver as Evie's dress. When I made it to his face, I noticed the intimate smile and sterling eyes that swirled like molten metal in the lighting. I only then registered the fact that he was dancing and flirting, with Abby draped at his side.

Lucas moved me off to the side of the dance floor just in time. I was about to be toppled over by one of the huge linemen and his date as they looped around. "Grace, snap out of it." Lucas looked behind him to see what had captured my attention so fully. His face grew angry when he saw Eli and Abby. He turned to me and positioned himself between us, successfully blocking my view.

I was about to tell him I wanted a drink when my necklace began to warm with its warning. I began looking around again searching for whatever it was that sounded the necklace's alarm.

"Grace..." Lucas pulled at me trying again to capture my attention. I turned and walked away toward Evie, searching for the threat. "Grace, wait. Where are you going?" Lucas hissed, as he trailed behind me like a puppy on a leash.

I saw it again, then, by the entrance. A huge cloud of black fog, thick and heavy, hung in the air, growing exponentially. Someone opened the door to walk outside, and the fog was sucked out with the air conditioning and back into the night.

I zigzagged my way past the incoming people, following far enough behind it not to be noticed. I rounded the corner toward the alley, between the side of the cafeteria and the back of the brick gym, and abruptly stopped.

I could hear voices coming from the back corner, but I couldn't make out what they were saying. I peered into the darkness, trying to see who was there. Hands reached and grabbed me from behind covering my mouth. Lucas had pulled me back from sight. "Grace, what do you think you're doing?" he hissed through his clenched teeth.

"I'm putting an end to this for good." I murmured as I pulled my arm out of his grip and my mouth away from his hands. I turned, trying to get back to the alley, but Lucas pulled me back around. He gently shoved me up against the wall and trapped me with his arms.

"I can't let you do that, Grace. It's suicide."

"It's not suicide, Lucas. It's my job." I tried to duck under his arms, but he stopped me with one of his large hands, effectively halting my getaway.

He pulled me back against the wall and leaned in so close that I could feel his warm breath on my face. I looked up into his eyes, trying to decipher what it was he was thinking.

He leaned in and whispered into my ear, "Someone is coming." I could hear footsteps in the grass. He was right, someone was approaching.

Before I realized what was happening, his mouth crashed into mine. My eyes widened and rounded at the contact. My hands went to his chest on their own volition. I tried to push him away, but it was like moving a mountain.

I curled my hands into a fist and furiously pounded at his chest, trying to make him let me go. As he stood there with his lips against mine and my trying to shove him away, I heard the approaching footsteps abruptly stop.

I heard the unmistakable intake of air, as someone gasped. I felt the tangible fracture of a heart as it echoed its broken beat in my own chest.

I sensed electricity charge the air and felt a chilling surge of wind blow past me, hard enough to knock Lucas away and onto the ground. Eli, succeeding where I had failed.

Lucas looked at me apologetically as he stood up and brushed himself off. I stood there hugging myself as Eli stared off into the air above us. His fist clenched and unclenched repeatedly. The muscles in his mouth worked overtime as he clamped and ground his teeth together.

Lucas tried to speak, but Eli's gaze snapped to him, and the looks we both gave him shut him up. Minutes passed as the three of us stood there, the tension thick like corded rubber, palpable and heavy.

Eventually Eli hung his head and muttered, "I knew there was something going on between the two of you." He tucked his hands into his pockets.

"Eli, it's not like that. Grace and I are partners. We..." Eli's attention snapped to him. His eyes narrowed skeptically as he took a step in Lucas's direction.

"Is that what we're calling this nowadays?"

Lucas raised his hands in surrender. "I don't want to fight with you, man."

"Then maybe you should have kept your hands away from Grace." Eli spat as he took another menacing step toward Lucas. Lucas ducked around Eli and started backing toward the gym.

"I'm walking away. We've all been friends for too long for you to do something stupid. But I need you to listen to what she tells you." He gestured to me.

Eli laughed scornfully. "Oh, you mean, like you kissing Grace, that kind of stupid?" Lucas just shook his head and walked away.

When he was out of sight, Eli turned to me. "What did you do to my sister?" he quizzed angrily.

"Evie? I didn't do anything to your sister..."

"Oh yeah," he interrupted, "...then why was she crying all day? Why did she drag me to the mall to find her a dress? And why weren't you there to help her get ready?"

I opened my mouth to answer and he shouted, "Why were you sneaking around and following us today?"

I tried to reply again when he continued his tirade. "I have to say, Grace, that's a bit low, even for you."

My own temper flared, and I cocked my head to the side. "Which part, Eli?" I stepped toward his towering frame.

"When Abby decided to crash our date?" I took another step to him "When you avoided me after that night? When you ignored me for an entire week, yet you flirted endlessly with Abby?"

Another step. "How about the fact that last night you begged me not to say anything to you that would hurt you, even though I really needed to tell you something. And, honestly, I don't have that kind of power over you. Then there is how you completely dismissed me today while you and Abby were cozy on the dance floor?"

I moved another step forward. "How about the fact that Lucas and I have saved you and your sister more times than you'll ever know?" I closed the distance peering up into his eyes.

He swallowed thickly, fighting his own temper as I continued "And what do I get in return, Eli? I get ignored by the only boy whose attention I actually want. And his sister, my only friend, becomes so angry with the truth that she pretends I don't exist." I uncrossed my arms and stood my ground.

"So tell me, which part is low, even for me? Which part did I have any control over?" Eli's mouth opened and closed, like a fish out of water, while he struggled for words.

I brushed him off. "You know what? No, whatever is about to come out of your mouth is only going to make me angrier." I shook my head and waved my hand in dismissal. "Just no. Let me say this..."

I paused to make sure he was listening, "You know, in your heart, that I didn't want Lucas to kiss me. You know it wasn't what it looked like. And you know there is no Lucas and me." I air quoted. "We work together; beyond that, we're just friends."

His eyes blazed. "Then why did you let him kiss you?" he took a step forward making me take a small step back to look up into his face.

"You know what? I don't even want to know that answer." He waved it off as if it were a swarm of gnats.

"I just have one more question." He thrust his hands through his hair and took a large step away from me. "Why were you following me?" he repeated through his clenched teeth.

"Because I was trying to protect you..." I tried to will enough force into my voice so that he'd believe me.

"I don't need your protection," he growled.

"It's my job!" I screamed furiously. Eli spun toward the front of the building, about to walk away from me.

"No," I shouted and reached to touch his arm. "You do not get to walk away from me, Eli. This..." The electricity that sparked at our contact shocked me, knocking me back several steps.

My back blazed with a fiery inferno. My mark began to glow. The alley appeared lit up, as if a night light had suddenly been plugged in.

An agonizing pulse began to pound against my spine, bending it in half as it grew persistent, beating faster and faster. It struck repeatedly until my body relented. It could no longer contain the enormity inside.

The creature that clawed my insides abruptly burst from my back, furiously in a majestic eruption of luminous color. Except what had erupted from within me wasn't a beast after all.

The alley suddenly looked as if it were daylight, brighter than a clear mid-afternoon. Twin, translucent wings unfurled and stretched from my back, as if they had been cramped in a tiny prison cell too long.

Light bounced through the feathers, refracting everywhere, as if each were a crystal prism. Rainbows of color cascaded down the brick wall of the gym, the soft green grass beneath my feet, and illuminated Eli's eternal silvery glow.

I reached to touch a wing, but my finger passed straight through it, intangibly, like a ray of light through a windowpane. While my wings moved, the opaque feathers tinkled lightly, like a glass chandelier in a passing breeze.

Eli's eyes widened as he stumbled backwards. I tried to reach for him. "Eli?" I pleaded but my voice sounded weird to my own ears, much like a tiny bell ringing.

I stepped forward toward him, but he scrambled back further and further, before taking off at a supernaturally paced sprint. He left me alone, confused and scared, standing in the alley.

Raguel materialized like a gentle comforting presence. He wore his true form, but it appeared dim and overshadowed, like when the sun passed behind a white puffy cloud. He had a smile on his face and placed a warm hand on my cheek. I tried to ask what was happening, but my mouth couldn't form words.

He looked behind me and spoke. "Take her home; she has drawn too much attention here. I will hold them off." Lucas guided me to his waiting truck and drove me home.

During the short ride home, I managed to fall asleep. I remembered the swaying sensation of being carried up the stairs. The feel of strong arms gripped me tightly and cradled me into a firm chest. The swaying motion soothingly rocked me into a deeper sleep. I awoke the next morning with my mother and Lucky snuggling me in my bed.

My wings had vanished while I slept.

CHAPTER TWENTY-THREE

I spent the following week at school avoiding two of my former best friends. The impending doom of the prophesy felt monstrous and violent. I could feel the tendrils of whatever was about to happen clawing up my spine. Sometimes its grip was visceral, choking me with its unease and momentarily paralyzing me with fear. Sometimes, I felt surer and more confident that we could defeat whatever was thrown at us.

Lucas and I snuck around after school protecting the twins while staying out of sight, working from within the shadows. We took turns on who watched them overnight, the other bringing espressos to help ward off the lack of slumber and the chilly fall air.

When they weren't together, we'd play Rock-paper-scissors on who covered whom. In the end, it didn't matter; we'd each be protecting one or the other, no matter what.

During the classes we shared with them, I made sure I was the last into the room. I sat the closest to the door in order to make the quickest exit. Sweeping the hall with my senses hunting for anything out of the ordinary.

In biology, Lucas and I sat at the front of the classroom. I could feel Eli's burning glare warming the back of my head, but I refused to relent. Our assigned seating went out the window long ago anyway.

Abby and her merry gang of doppelgängers were unusually quiet after the homecoming dance. I was thankful that they chose to leave me alone now. I didn't have the energy to refute whatever brutality they decided to dish this week.

Instead of eating lunch inside the cafeteria with the group, Lucas and I chose a spot outside in the courtyard but close enough to sense trouble.

When I wasn't at school or stalking my former friends, I was at GUESS training with my newly birthed wings. They were weightless and moved faster than my body or my mind could.

I continually found myself stabbing through them or stepping on them. Raguel was patient with me, something that was truly at odds with his personality. It didn't take me long before I was able to go through traditional training exercises without a blunder.

Friday was an important day. Well, important to me anyway. It was my birthday. I followed what had become my normal routine for that week. At lunch, Lucas held out a large pink-frosted cupcake, contained inside a cellophane box.

"Happy Birthday, Grace," he exclaimed.

I smiled up at him brilliantly. "Thank you, Lucas." He pulled out two forks and sat down to help me eat it. The weather had turned bitingly cold overnight, unusual for that time of year.

We were the only two in the courtyard, but I lowered my voice anyway. "Any news?" This was a new ritual I had begun sometime after the dance. I seemed to need constant reassurance that everything was ok.

Lucas frowned and sighed heavily. "No, nothing new has been reported." He cut another piece of cupcake with his fork. "Grace, it's your birthday. It's okay to enjoy it." He took a bite.

I nodded my head in agreement, though I wasn't sure I was. I felt like a walking mound of mismatched puzzle pieces. Everything I had known—the life I had known—had been tossed into the air and left to land as it scattered in the wind. I didn't know how my life would turn out now. The unknown frightened and intimidated me.

An icy breeze blew the hair off my neck. I shivered as I ducked down inside my coat.

"I think we should go in; lunch is almost over." Lucas proclaimed as he popped the lid back on the box and took our trash to the nearest can.

We walked inside and almost right into Eli and Evie in a heated debate in front of the cafeteria doors. We had stopped too fast.

I lurched forward, my feet caught, and I tripped on the rubber floor mat like a new-born baby giraffe, sending me right into Eli's waiting arms.

He caught me, stopping my fall before I landed on the floor in yet another embarrassing incident for the record books. I righted myself and adjusted my jacket.

"Thanks," I muttered, as I slung my heavy backpack onto my shoulders.

We stood there looking into each other's eyes for several minutes. I wanted him to say something, anything, to make this awful ache in my chest go away. I willed him to tell me anything. Anything at all. But he didn't.

Evie looked between the two of us and rolled her eyes. In a huff she threw her arms up into the air and stormed off.

Lucas shuffled beside me, obviously, uncomfortable with the overcast tension.

I broke eye contact to watch her go. My breath hitched, and I wondered if this would ever be right again. I turned in the opposite direction Evie had just left and practically ran out of the cafeteria.

The rest of the afternoon was gloomy. The happiness of it being both Friday and my birthday was overshadowed by the longing in my heart.

I trudged myself up the stairs and threw open the door of my bedroom. I decided I would clean it. Not that it was messy, it just gave me something to do.

However, when the door thumped the wall, I noticed that on my bed sat a large box wrapped in pink and silver wrapping paper. A satiny pink ribbon wove around the box and was tied together on top in a loopy bow. Tucked into the folds of the ribbon was a card.

I plucked the card off the package. A silver and pink teddy bear adorned the front of the white card stock.

Inside the card read:

My Dearest Grace,

Happy 17th birthday, sweetheart.

I dropped the card onto my bed. No one had signed it, but I knew that the scrawled words on the paper were not in my mother's handwriting.

I picked up the box and began to untie the ribbon. Mom appeared in the doorway holding a package similar to the one I held. "Oh, someone beat me to it." She entered the room and set her present on the dresser next to me. "Well, who is it from?" she cooed. I waved her over and handed her the card, the box still perched on my lap.

She read the card and inhaled air like a vacuum cleaner, her eyes going wide. She clutched the card to her chest. When she sat down, it wasn't gentle like normal. Instead, she plopped down hard and on the edge of the bed making it flop and bounce like a trampoline.

"Dad?" I asked, though I really didn't need to. The look on her face was proof enough.

She cleared her throat. "Well, open it," she said breathlessly. I raised my eyes at her, doubting her sanity.

I unfolded the rest of the ribbon and tucked it behind us. Then, I tore into the shiny silver and pink paper. An unmarked white box lay inside. I pried the lid off with a suctioned pop of static only to be greeted by white tissue paper.

I unfolded the layers and layers of paper before finally revealing a white long-sleeved cardigan sweater. It had crystal beading sewn onto the edges of the neck and sleeves. It was soft, like cashmere, but smooth, like the softest silk.

"That's beautiful," my mother said dumbfounded, as she swiped a stray tear from her cheek.

I laid it back into the box and set it aside as she shoved her present into my hands. "Here open mine now." She beamed at me. I went through the motions of carefully opening a present for the second time. This time though, inside lay a light-yellow sundress with eyelet-laced trimming and tiny white embroidered flowers scattered sparsely over the remainder of the dress.

"I bought this for you to wear to your party tonight. But I'm not sure we should have one." She patted my hand for comfort. "How about you and I go out for dinner to celebrate instead?"

"That sounds like a great idea, Mom." I leaned over and gave her a hug. "Thank you for the lovely dress and for planning what I am sure would have been the birthday party of the century."

She kissed my cheek. "Anything for you, baby. Now, go get dressed; I'm going to take you somewhere fancy."

I laughed to myself as I watched her waltz out of the room.

I was finishing slipping on my new dress when the doorbell rang. It rang again shortly after I had swiped the last bit of mascara on my eyelashes. And yet again as I slid on my new cardigan and sandals.

I walked downstairs and into a full-blown party. I looked at my mother, who sheepishly shrugged her shoulders.

Lucas was helping my mom hang balloons and a birthday banner. Party trays of snacks had been set out and arranged on the bar-top counter.

On the stove, sat a two-tiered white frosted cake with pink flowers draped down the cake like a waterfall. Pink candles in the shape of the number seventeen poked out of the top like twin sparklers.

There were so many people from school there. I wasn't friends with any of them, but they all had shown up anyway.

Music blasted from the living room speakers. People were everywhere. I shoved my way over to Lucas and my mom.

"Why are all of these people here?" I asked wide-eyed.

Lucas laughed as he gestured to encompass the enormity of the crowd. "This is what happens when your mom posts a flyer on the cork board in the courtyard at the school." He elbowed me while he poked fun at my mom.

I glared at him and raised an eyebrow while crossing my arms in front of my chest. He ducked guiltily out of the path of my eyes' laser beams.

My mom turned and grimaced when something fell off a shelf in the living room, landing with a glass-shattering crash.

"Oh, honey, I'm sorry. It's just you and Evie are in that little tiff and she had promised to hand out invites. I just thought this would be the next best thing. I meant to take it down...I thought I had." She gestured to the room as something else was knocked down and broken. She closed her eyes and inhaled through her nose. "Obviously not."

"Nope." I let the "p" sound pop for emphasis.

I jumped as someone tapped my shoulder. I turned around to see who it was only to look into a familiar pair of silver eyes. "Evie?" My voice rose in question.

She looked down and shuffled her feet. "Um, can we talk?"

I shook my head "Yeah, sure. Come on." I gestured up the stairs so that we would have some privacy.

When I closed the door to my room behind me, Evie raced over and pulled me into a hug. "I'm so sorry." She tightened the hug.

"Grace, I'm scared." She pulled away.

Tears brimmed in her eyes as she dropped onto the bed disturbing Lucky's party escape.

I sat down next to her absently stroking his soft little head. "Me too."

She shook her head, "Grace, what I saw. It's…" she trailed off her eyes looking far away at nothing, "…it's coming for us. All of us. This entire world." She turned to me, eyes rounded with horror. "It's terrifying, Grace."

"I know." I said again, comforting her.

She looked down into her lap and closed her hands. "I've always known about you. I see you in my visions often. You're so shiny." She swallowed.

"I knew about Eli and Lucas, too. But I didn't know how big this was." She picked at a cuticle. "I thought we were some mutant freaks with cool abilities. I didn't know."

She shook her head and closed her eyes, tears streaking her cheeks. "I'm sorry. Can you forgive me, Grace?"

I smiled and pulled her into a one-armed hug. "Of course, I forgive you, Evie." She sniffled and smiled back at me.

After a few minutes, I smiled again for a completely different reason. "You know, I'm kind of glad we don't belong with the X-Men, even though Professor X was a sweet guy."

Evie burst out laughing, her ribs shaking trying to get enough air into her lungs. "You know what, though? He did love kids, and that's important in a guy," she said through her panting.

Her laugh was contagious. I found myself laughing until tears ran down my cheeks.

When we finally had composed ourselves enough, I stood and extended my hand to help her up. "Let's go eat some cake".

Mom smiled an enormous smile when she saw the two of us walking back down the stairs.

"Cake, cake, cake," the room chanted.

She turned and put the cake on the table.

"Let's light these candles, shall we?" Mom said. She searched a couple of drawers before she found the lighter and pulled it out.

I blew out my candles to a chorus of mostly strangers singing me Happy Birthday.

When we had finished eating, I unwrapped presents thanking everyone for their gift. Evie had bought us matching silver braided rings. They were bent and twisted with a knot in the middle. Evie called them Friendship Knot rings. They were beautiful and dainty. The party then wound down, most of the crowd had dispersed.

I was talking with Oliver; Lucas and Evie were laughing at some random joke Ollie had said when Eli finally came and found me.

"About time," Evie muttered quietly under her breath. That received chuckles of agreement with the other two boys. Eli threw daggers at all three of them.

He tucked his hands into his pockets and nodded toward the sliding glass door that led from the kitchen to the backyard patio. "Can I have a minute?" he asked.

I sat my drink down on the counter and walked to the coat rack. I pulled my discarded new cardigan off a hook and wrapped myself in it. Eli slid the door open and gestured for me to go through first.

The breezy air hit me in the face just before the glowing white Christmas lights, twinkling from the patio and tied to the old oak tree in the middle of the back yard, caught my attention.

My sandaled feet kicked leaves up and made them stick in my shoes, as I ventured further into the yard. Eli, crunching leaves under feet, was not far behind.

When I felt I had wandered far enough, I whipped around to challenge him, my arms crossed waiting for him to speak. He came to an abrupt stop behind me.

He looked me up and down as if making sure I was okay. I guess, supposing the last time he truly had seen me, it was an expected reaction. I wasn't exactly in normal condition then.

I raised my eyebrows expecting him to speak, growing more impatient. I knew whatever this was, I wasn't going to enjoy it. And I surely wasn't going to start this sordid conversation.

He huffed out his breath as he rubbed the back of his neck and looked toward the sky.

After a few moments of our standing there, I decided I'd had enough. I started for the house.

"Grace," his voice croaked. His pleading tone stopped me where I stood.

There we were balancing on a knife's edge, halfway between the door and the tree. I felt like a puppet on a string, dangling unnoticed until he decided to pick up my strings again.

"This isn't going to work, Eli." I shook my head, refusing to turn around and look at him. I knew that if I did look at him, this would hurt me so much worse.

"What isn't going to work?" His voice broke.

"You and me; it won't work." I called backwards over my shoulder. I held onto my courage, trying not to let any tears fall from my eyes. It was agony, pure and simple. When I felt I had enough strength to walk away, I went to do just that.

Eli grabbed my elbow and turned me flush to him. He tilted my chin up so he could look me in the eyes, his fingers barely touching me.

"Not going to work?" He tried to puzzle the meaning behind those four words. Whatever conclusion he drew from them made him laugh a little manically and shake his head "Not going to work? Grace, You and me..." he gestured to us both. "...We were written in the stars."

I tried to pull away from him, but he closed the distance again.

My temper burned. "Oh yeah? Written in the stars, you say? Right. Which part of the stars, Eli? The third that fell or the rest that are left? Because I know…" His lips collided into mine, effectively silencing my rant.

His warm hands cupped my face gently. It was as if the kiss were the bandage our souls needed to piece themselves back together after we had so thoroughly ripped them apart.

He tasted like mint and cake. It was the second time a boy had kissed me and the only time I felt the zinging sparks that set the butterflies in my stomach a flight.

I had loved this boy for as long as I could remember. He had broken my heart repeatedly; yet, here I still stood, in the cold air under the canopy of twinkling lights giving in to the gentle brush of his kiss against my lips.

He broke our kiss and leaned his forehead against mine. His body rigid with fear. I closed my eyes as a tear dripped down my chin and landed with a plop on the grass.

He kissed my forehead and stepped away. "I'm sorry..." He swallowed thickly. The anguish I felt in my soul, emerging in his voice, "...I couldn't think of the right words to make you stay. I couldn't find the words to tell you that I was sorry. That I was wrong. I messed everything up with you, Grace."

He thrust a hand through his hair and sighed. "And I couldn't stop thinking about kissing you. In fact, it's all I have been able to think about lately. So, instead of wishing I could, I just did."

He tucked his hands into his jean pockets. "If you are going to walk away because I was stupid, I needed to know what it could have been like between us. I'm begging you, Grace; please don't walk away."

I stood there as silent tears fell from my eyes. "I can't," I whispered, as I turned to look at the dying party happening through the glass panes.

The little hope he had left deflated like a popped balloon. "Please, don't," he whispered. "I just need one date. One real date to show you that this will work."

"I can't keep doing this, Eli. It hurts too much." I pointed to my heart.

We stood there for some time with our hearts exposed, silence hung heavy in the air.

"Do you know the first day I knew that I loved you?" he asked.

I sniffled and shook my head no.

"The day I met you." He gently took my hand.

"I'm not trying to be cheesy. It's true. We were five, but you were the brightest thing I had ever seen. You were so luminating and brilliant, like a neon sign in the middle of the Sahara Desert. This light radiated within you and shined so bright it was like looking at a thousand suns. When you smiled, I knew that I was a goner." He squeezed my fingers.

"Not one bit of this whole *save the world thing,* you have going on surprises me." His lips tilted in a half-shrugged grin.

"I never asked for this, Eli." I said, trying to wiggle a leaf from my sandal, anything to keep this conversation at bay.

"No, maybe you didn't but, it's yours anyway." Silence stretched taught between us.

"You know, Grace, ever since I met you, you've tried to hide in the corner of a circular room. But the fact is, when you walk into a room, everyone notices you. You're so bright it's impossible not to." He ground a leaf under the toe of his boot, never once letting go of my hand.

"So, at the risk of being told no again, may I please take you out tomorrow night?" he blushed as he asked again.

I smiled a little nervously. "Only if we can go back inside. It's freezing out here." His laugh echoed and bounced around on the backyard fence panels.

CHAPTER TWENTY-FOUR

Evie ended up staying the night when the birthday party ended. The next day, she took me shopping and bought me yet another dress for a birthday present. I tried to tell her that it was too much, but she just brushed me off, saying something under her breath about "no fashion sense."

This dress was an emerald-green, fitted, wrap dress that ended at the knee. It was made of a soft cotton. Its sleeves ended about mid arm. Perfect for this cool evening. She paired the dress with my tall leather boots and buttery smooth jacket. I wore my hair down and straight, with just a hint of makeup.

Eli knocked on the door, punctual as usual. Before we walked out the door, Evie called out to us. She'd only taken a single step down the stairs. "Hey! You guys eat inside tonight. The weather is going to turn bad and you don't want to be anywhere near the roof top."

Eli shot her a look to hush her before she ruined my surprise.

"I'm sorry, it's just…it's going to get dark fast." Her eyes widened and looked directly at me. "You don't like the dark, right, Grace?"

It was an odd question, but I answered anyway "No, Evie, I don't like the dark; you're right."

She swallowed and looked to the bottom of the steps drumming her fingers on the banister. "Just don't touch it. And don't go into it. You'll be okay then." She rushed back up the stairs and to my room.

I looked at Eli. He shrugged as if this was normal behavior for his sister. I knew better. I wanted to go to her and ask what was wrong, but Eli touched my arm. "We have to go, Grace, if you want to make it to the restaurant on time."

I rolled my eyes. "Mr. Punctuality," I said, as I glanced back up the stairs for one last fleeting look at Evie before I brushed past him and to his car. He chuckled as he climbed in.

It took thirty to forty minutes to make it into downtown Houston. There was always road construction, accidents, and traffic. Houston also could have been considered a city that never slept. It seemed as if people were always coming, going, or just passing through on their way to somewhere else. I looked up into the street lamps to watch as they ticked by.

Before long, the tale-tale skyscrapers made their presence known. I looked to Eli, who was so focused on the road. He didn't notice that my attention had turned to him.

The dashboard's glow reflected his strong profile. He had one hand resting on the armrest, as if waiting for me to decide if I wanted contact with him; his other perched on the steering wheel.

I smiled to myself and gently placed my small hand into his waiting larger one. He flashed me a smile and pumped our connected hands. Then he visibly relaxed his posture, as if he'd been waiting on me to decide if I was in this or not.

I didn't go into the big city often. It always amazed me to see the buildings stretching so high into the air that it seemed whoever originally designed them was trying to make contact with God. Funny that they didn't realize, you don't have to be close to the sky to talk to him.

Eli pulled up to a covered walkway. A valet was waiting to take his keys and drive the car for parking. He ran around my side of the car and opened the door for me. We walked into the building arm and arm.

Inside the massive hotel on the twenty second floor, was a sophisticated restaurant. A portion sat inside the hotel enclosed in an all-encompassing room with a three-hundred-and-sixty-degree glass view of the city below.

The other portion of the restaurant was on the roof top, a whole twenty-three floors up, with an open view of the sky and city sprawling beneath.

We took the elevator up to the twenty-second floor. Eli gave his name to the hostess and asked for a seat inside. I glanced around the room and realized there wouldn't be any seating left. I tugged Eli's hand. "The restaurant is full. Look," I said to him.

The hostess hung up the phone on her stand and looked at Eli. "Mr. Cole, I apologize; we only have available seating on the roof top tonight."

Eli's head whipped to me. I shrugged my shoulders. The air outside was fine and the sky looked clear. He turned back to her "Okay, we'll take it."

The hostess smiled, looking a bit relieved. "Okay, great. They're waiting for you upstairs; enjoy your dinner."

We made our way up the curved flight of stairs, our boots pounding and echoing as we climbed. Other restaurant patrons were coming and going. We were almost to the top when someone bumped into me, making me stumble and step down a few steps to keep from falling.

"Sorry, miss," the clumsy waiter said. He looked familiar, but I couldn't place where I'd seen him. The now familiar feeling of alarm slammed into me. It worked its way up my spine, scrabbling with its hooks and making me shiver, before settling like a sunken ship in the bottom of my stomach.

Eli took my hand, drawing my attention back to him. "You okay?" he asked.

"Yep, A okay," I said, as we finally made it to the top.

The rooftop restaurant had a glass fence around the edge. Propane-fueled patio heaters had been brought out and lit making the area warm.

A brick bar sat to the right of the entrance, where guests comfortably sat on plush couches and barstools. We were led away from the bar toward the opposite side of the restaurant and seated.

Not many people had elected to eat up top, but they were missing out on the best view, in my opinion. Glass tables lined the area, with lighted candles casting a soft glow over the restaurant.

We looked over the menu. Eli tried to make pleasant conversation, but I couldn't engage. I felt as if the other shoe was about to drop. I couldn't release the feeling that we were on a pinnacle about to plummet into whatever awaited us. Eli dropped his menu. "Grace?" he puzzled, drawing his brow in question.

"It's okay, Eli." I smiled, trying not to show the fear I truly felt was eating me alive from the inside.

The waiter came and took our order. The same waiter who had brushed me in the hallway almost sending me toppling down. Once again, I had this sense that I knew him from somewhere.

He was young, maybe college-aged. He was tall and thin. His amber hair was long on top but cut short underneath. The long part of his hair was tied in a knot at the back of his head. He had sleepy, blue eyes under a thick brow. A pair of small, plump lips rested under his proportionate nose. He had a strong, masculine jawline, with a prominent Adam's apple on his thin, corded neck. He was handsome and striking.

I must have sat there looking at him a little too long. Eli cleared his throat, raising his eyebrows in question. I looked away and shook my head to clear it. "I'm sorry; what was your question?"

The waiter, whose golden name tag read Uri, asked again, "What can I get you to drink?"

I blinked, still not registering or answering the question. Eli sighed, "She'll have a glass of water now and a Coke with dinner." Uri wrote it on his note pad.

Still dazed, I didn't register the rest of the order Eli had placed. When the waiter reached for my menu, I saw a flash of a tattoo in the palm of his right hand. My heart sped up. Two stars were conspicuously etched into his pale skin.

I glanced up to his eyes as he was bent forward reaching toward me. His eyes glinted in the light before he gently removed my menu from my hands. I watched until he disappeared from view.

Eli grabbed my hand across the table, drawing my attention back to him. "If I were insecure, I'd say you were making googley eyes at our waiter." He laughed in disbelief.

I smiled at him with softening words. "No, that's not it. I just had this feeling that I know him, but I couldn't place where from." I squeezed Eli's hand.

"I've been wondering something." Eli patiently waited for me to continue. "Why did you run away from me the night of the homecoming dance?"

His face flushed, and he hung his head. "I really don't have a good reason, Grace." He reached up and rubbed the back of his neck. "Evie had just told me what had—had her so terrified before we went to decorate; and then when I saw you in the alley with these enormous wings, I panicked and ran. All I could think was the nightmare Evie had told me was true."

He looked up at me with wide eyes. "It wasn't you I ran from. I ran from the truth."

I tilted my head in question. "What did Evie tell you?" Our order arrived at that moment, releasing him from having to answering the question.

A plate with a small steak, mashed potatoes, and artfully arranged thin carrots was set before each of us. Fluffy and dense dinner rolls were served in a basket with easily spreadable, softened butter.

We ate and enjoyed our small talk about school and football. We talked about pretty much everything under the sun. It was easy and fun being with Eli like this. I felt myself growing more and more relaxed as the evening went on.

Eventually, Eli paid our check and excused himself from the table. The waiter came back with our receipt, but with Eli absent, he handed it to me. Once again, his palm flashed me as he handed me the check. This time there was only one star.

Peculiarly, I remembered there being two earlier. I scrunched my face up puzzled and looked to the unique waiter about to ask where it was, but Eli had returned.

I glanced down toward his outstretched hand, the tattoo in his palm once again showing two stars.

Chills raced against my skin, raising the hair on my arms and at the back of my neck.

I lifted widened eyes up to him when my necklace began to warm. "Eli," I whispered hoarsely.

Time slowed to a crawl.

Eli stood halfway between sitting and standing. The waiter paused mid turn, leaving us behind and the inky darkness stretching its fingers toward Eli.

"No!" I roared, as my sword flashed into place wrapping around my hand in its delicate gauntlet and blazing light.

I abruptly stood and put myself between Eli and those talons of darkness.

A cackling laugh sent the darkness swirling like smoke. Abby materialized from within it. She swirled her finger in the air, making time move again at normal speed.

"Oh, dear Grace, you stupid, stupid, girl." She flashed her teeth, eyes darkening like burnt ash.

"I had thought that your friend Lucas was the foretold light bearer. Little did I know it would be you, pipsqueak. Such a mighty task for such a little mouse." She tisked. "You can imagine my surprise when you nicked me at school the other day."

"That was you?" I asked through gritted teeth, still trying to puzzle out what was going on.

I reached back with my free hand to touch Eli. He had stood and turned to look at the now violent scene before us, shock written on his face. "Abby?" he asked.

She swung her long blonde hair over her shoulder and rolled her eyes. "You know, I really hate that name. My name is Abaddon."

She quickly ducked around me, reaching for Eli, but I flashed the sword her direction "I don't think so, Abby," I cooed tauntingly, drawing her attention back to me. When I made sure she was focused on me, I made my move.

I arched the sword down as a pointed bit of darkness jutted out from behind her, leaking toward Eli.

A tiny fragile hand reached through the thick substance for Eli. On its ring finger, rested a thin knotted ring. The twin to my own. My eyes rounded in terror.

"Evie?" I gasped

Abby reached into the darkness and pulled Evie out with a cackling, wicked laugh.

"Grace," she murmured before she went completely limp. Evie looked wretched. A thick coating of oily slime was smeared over her entire body. Her hair was matted and stuck to her face. Messy splashes of goop stuck to her clothes and she wasn't wearing any shoes.

"What did you do to her?" I shouted at Abby.

"Nothing that wasn't supposed to happen to her. But it's cute you actually thought you could stop this." She leered.

"Apollyon, take the boy; I'll deal with the rodent," she said, talking to the black cloud dripping with a plop onto the concrete like pudding.

"Apollyon, is my twin brother, you see. We've been doing this for what seems to be an eternity. Seduce the men, kill the protector. Blah, blah, blah. It's my job, but it gets a bit boring after a couple of centuries." She mock-picked at something on her nails.

She laughed again. "I am so glad the big birds in the sky decided to send me a female to kill, as if you would be a worthy opponent. You're so tiny." she said as she held up two fingers and pinched them together.

Evie's head lulled to the side; Abby seemed to consider her a moment before she continued her speech. "So, Apollyon might have smothered her light too much; like all boys he can be a bit dense," she said as if I would agree with her and any of this made sense. She flung Evie's lifeless body into a nearby chair.

"I think the only one dense is you Abby." I spat as I whipped out with the sword and nicked her in the arm again. Then I lunged toward Evie.

Abby sucked in a hiss of air. "You're going to pay for that one, squeaks." She made squealing noises, taunting me, as blackened ink poured from the gash in her sleeve.

The wind lifted my hair and tossed it about. I knew then that Eli was using his powers. I only had a quick glance at him as he fought his own nightmarish creature.

It had the body of a man but was a solid void, as black as a starless sky, dripping and reforming itself continuously. Eli tried to use his powers over the laws of nature, but he was new and untrained.

Each time he sent a thundering bolt of lightning at the form, it would explode its vulgar tar everywhere, decaying anything it hit. Eli couldn't duck out of the way fast enough to miss the exploded globs.

Each one that pelted him stuck like gum to his skin, fusing with him and weakening him. Before long, he too was held prisoner by the monstrous creature, just like his sister.

"Your turn, little Gracie." Abby jeered. The sword had other ideas. Without warning, I stabbed at Abby. She sent a massive ball of oozing black goo at me that I dodged easily.

"Oh come on, Abby; you can do better than that." I mocked as I tried to scrabble toward Eli and Evie, but I couldn't make it far enough.

She sent another and then another one right after the other. Each one slapped the brick behind me with a sickening slurp, causing the bricks and deck to age rapidly before crumbling.

We played this game for what seemed like hours. Me trying to inject her with the sword; her trying to hit me with the black substance.

Before long, the building began to quake. People ran from the rooftop, screaming as if just now realizing the spectacle wasn't a dinner show. Someone pulled the fire alarm evacuating the building. The sirens pierced the air, deafening my ears.

It was at that moment that Eli managed to wipe enough goop off himself. He called on the storms and the wind, creating a funnel cloud large enough to encompass the entire downtown Houston skyline.

My eyes rounded in fear. There was absolutely no way he could control the storm. It spun faster and faster, whipping chairs and tables off the roof.

Abby advanced again; this time, she flicked thin onyx tendrils out like a whip, lashing my wrist. I felt it sliding up my skin like a leach sucking out my light from within me.

She struck me again, lashing me with her whips, gulping in my powers. Each time she hit me, I felt weaker. The storm was raging above us; the funnel cloud was almost touching land. Nearby buildings were rocking and swaying. Cars were flying through the air. Trees and power lines snapped in half.

Eli absorbed the sparking electricity and sent it toward Abby. She landed with a sickening thud against the wall. Eli raced to me, helping me wipe away the stains of the ebony sludge. I tried to tell him to get Evie and escape, but the onyx man leapt toward Eli. I rolled in front of him as it crashed into me.

Too late, I noticed it had succeeded in knocking Eli off his feet just as the swirling vortex of clouds passed by. I watched in horror as he was sucked off the roof. I tried to reach and grab him, but I was too slow. The muck had eaten too much of my light.

I crawled toward Evie fighting the push of wind against my body, trying to make it to her before she was sucked into it too. But I was too late for her as well.

I had to watch as the churning mass of clouds passed by and the black monstrosity Abby had called Apollyon tossed my best friend over the ledge. Her lifeless body spun in the vortex.

A tear streamed past my downcast head, as the realization hit me; they both were gone.

The monster swallowed Abby where she lay unconscious before it melted into a puddle of gunk and poured itself along the building, sending old decayed glass wood and brick to the ground in crumbling, deteriorated heaps.

I held on to the glass railing to keep myself upright and on the roof, but the puddle of gore had touched the railing.

I lurched over the edge as the glass shattered to dust in front of me. I fell faster than the ink could dive. I reached to touch Eli, who was hanging onto a window ledge by his bloody fingertips. I was momentarily relieved that he was safe. As soon as I thought those words and he stretched his hand to mine, he was struck by falling debris. We both plummeted toward the ground. The thick shadow reached out and swallowed Eli whole.

Suddenly, I remembered the sword fixed firmly in my palm. I thrust it as hard as I could into the darkness and through the building trying to slow my fall. The black liquid covered the sword. I felt the metal gauntlet snap in two from around my wrist. The sword was forcefully stuck into the building, but I continued to drop. The sword had released me, drained of its power.

My wings burst from my back cocooning me in their shell as I landed in the middle of the busy asphalted street, creating a massive crater in the ground from the concussive blow to the earth and a crack up the now half-toppled building.

I lay there with tears scalding my cheeks and watched in horror as Eli was carried away, wrapped within the liquid nightmare.

I closed my eyes as sobs began to wrack my bruised body. I had failed. I tried to stand, but I found that I didn't have the strength. I lay in the crater staring at the sword imbedded hilt-deep within the brick façade.

A blinding light made me close my eyes. When I opened them again, the waiter was standing there with his right hand extended toward me and his left toward the sword.

One star lay in his right palm. "Noohra come." He spoke, and the sword began to rattle and vibrate before releasing from its trap and floating into his outstretched hand. Traces of the oozing darkness still defiled its hilt. He shook it to try and release it, but it didn't budge. He then brought it to his mouth and blew on the sword. The darkness crumbled like ash and scattered in the wind.

My eyes widened with recognition as I remembered then where I had seen him before. He was the new teacher's aide at the high school, the same one who had run into the darkness just a few weeks before. He looked back at me and shook his head to silence me. "Now is not the time," he said, as I grabbed his hand. He shocked me with his power, rejuvenating my faded light.

When he'd helped me to stand, he commanded, "Go. Retrieve them," as he clasped the sword Noohra around my neck.

I stretched my wings to their full extent making the feathers clink together like crystal and sending rainbows of light bouncing around the street.

I remembered then Evie's earlier warning and strange behavior. "You don't like the darkness do you Grace...just don't touch it and don't go into it. You'll be all right." My wings flexed and as I heaved into the air, a shockwave of sound shattered every nearby window.

My wings effortlessly carried me as I chased the fading darkness set on doing just that. I knew two things for certain. I would have done anything to have saved them. And I would have my revenge.

TURN THE NEXT PAGE FOR A SNEAK PEEK OF BOOK TWO...

THE REALM OF DUALITY

RELEASING TBA 2019

COPYRIGHT © 2018 by Patricia D. Adams

THE REALM OF DUALITY

THE PATRIARCHS COVENANT SERIES BOOK TWO

PATRICIA D. ADAMS

CHAPTER ONE

For the last week, I had awoken to sweat-soaked sheets; small gashes and cuts along my arms, hands, legs and feet; and haunting nightmares of torture and gore. The feeling of malevolence permeated my waking thoughts and chased me into slumber. I had assumed it was from flailing in my restless sleep and running from my nightmares. These last few months had been anything but easy.

However, this morning my assumption was proven wrong. The large gash that ran along my abdomen to my hip, had seeped thick dark blood through my bed clothes and sheets. The silver hilted sword I kept on a chain around my neck was embedded in my headboard inches above my sleeping head.

And then, there was what appeared to be a dead angel on my bedroom floor, oddly splayed like a bear skinned rug. A loud snore rumbled through the room. Not dead then. Just injured.

"Good morning, why are you here?" My sleep-thick voice sounded too cheery to even my own ears. The angel growled at me by way of morning greeting. So that was great, a large extremely grumpy, injured angel was asleep on my bedroom floor. I sighed, heaved myself out of bed, and hobbled to my bathroom.

I pulled my tank away, peeking with one eye in the mirror as I tugged, flaking the drying blood as it pulled my shirt tight. The slice was already healing, thanks to my blessed ancestry and God-kissed brow. But alas, it was another set of PJs and sheets to be thrown away. Unfortunately, the ribbons and shredded slices in them made them unsalvageable.

Had you asked me six months ago if I thought this would be the norm, I'd have laughed right in your face. I grabbed a washcloth, cleaned the still-healing cut, threw on a pair of jeans and a t-shirt, and went to check on Lucas, whose sleeping form still was taking up what little space I had for a bedroom floor.

I toed him in the side. "Hey, sleepy head. Wake up" He grumbled something incoherent and rolled the other way. I shook him again, this time more forcefully, and huffed my annoyance out loud. "Lucas, just what are you doing on my bedroom floor?"

"Shhhhhhh," he grumped back at me.

"Lucas, get up," I demanded. He tried and failed miserably to rise from the carpeted floor. That's when I finally got a good look at his poor assaulted body.

His normally perfectly-combed hair hung limply in his eyes. His right eye was purple and had swollen completely shut. He had a gash in his forehead that ran to his bottom lip, which was also split wide open. He looked as if he had taken a sword to the face. Unfortunately, that wasn't the worst of it. He was barefoot and shirtless. His back muscles bunched with the effort to rise.

His jeans were ripped and sliced at odd intervals, blood oozing between each cut. His bare chest had a twin slice to my own across his rib cage. But where mine had sealed shut, his was wide open and pouring blood out in rivulets. I instantly was on my knees helping him to rise.

"We need to get you help," I stated. He finally lifted his one good eye to meet mine.

"No help," he forced out between clenched teeth.

"We need to get you cleaned off then." He sighed and resigned himself to being treated and hopefully healed. I wasn't as good as he was with the healing touch, but then, I'd only had my powers for six short months. You can't blame a girl for not knowing what she's doing just yet.

I had been practicing using my other gifts in the time since that horrific night. The ones that didn't require fighting.

Lucas was determined to throw himself at the worst of the darkness as if fighting could eat away his pain. I, however, changed my approach from day to day. Some days, I'd lay in bed and dream of the other life—the one where I had my best friend and her brother, the one that had been stolen from me. Other days, I'd throw myself into practicing weaponry and fighting. Lucas and I were fighting the darkness more often than not. But most days I avoided it all, determined to disengage from my emotions. I didn't want to feel. Feeling meant pain. Feeling meant tears. Feelings wouldn't help them now.

We had taken residence at GUESS when it had become ever so clear that I had failed miserably to stop the last holy war and prevent the death of my best friend and her twin brother. Or as the prophesy had called them, the prophet and the law giver. It was too late for that now, though. Grief was a horrid thing. It was a beast that chewed at your insides and never let go once it wormed its way into your heart.

I often found myself calling out to them as if they were still alive and well. The angels still wanted to retrieve their bodies for some morbid reason, and they claimed I was the one who would have to bring them home, a job I protested having to do almost daily.

I also was learning how to recover my light after the dark ick lashed out and clung to me, something that would have helped me to save Evie and Eli. The thought of their names sent a fresh wave of nauseating pain through my heart, making me gasp.

I helped Lucas to the bathroom. I healed the worst of the damages before my light started to wane. I sent pulses of light into the slices and gashes on his body. The light was brilliant and blinding, but I had been using too much lately.

"I'm sorry, Lucas, that's the best I can do for now." He grumbled something I couldn't decipher. I assumed it was,

Thank you, Grace, for all of your infinite help. I would be dead by now too if it weren't for you. But it was likely something along the lines of. You're weak and naïve; stop the inner monologue and get help.

Four months earlier, I had failed. Four months earlier, people I loved had died. I tried to chase the darkness, but I was too weak and frail from my fight with Abaddon and Apollyon. I made it almost halfway around the world before I fell to plummet the earth once again. My light had given out, as it was nearly all spent.

Raguel found me unconscious and frozen on a mountain several weeks later. I didn't know until I had awoken in my room at GUESS that it was possible for an angel to lose its light. I had almost died as well.

I had also learned then that I had failed in my mission. At that time, I began to wail with my grief and sobbed uncontrollably for days. I refused to eat. I refused to move. I refused to live.

Lucas pulled me back to the land of the living when he told me that Evie and Eli's parents were holding off on the funeral until they could find their bodies. That seemed to snap me out of it with a renewed sense of vengeance.

I lowered Lucas onto my bed and ran to his room grabbing new clothes for him. Sweat pants and a tank, easier to pull on and easier to change when the bandages needed later. By the time I had made it back to my room, Lucas was unconscious again. I left his fresh set of clothes at the foot of my bed and went to get help.

I refused to go into the dreamscape. I was furious with God. I needed him, and he didn't step in. So, if he was waiting for me to call on him, well he could just stop. I didn't want to talk to him. I didn't want to look into his glowing eyes. I didn't want another painful lesson on humanities frailty. I just wanted to slaughter the darkness. If one more person told me everything happens for a reason, I would scream.

I found Raguel in the security room, watching tapes from the human world—newscasts of some city with major damages. I paid it no attention and turned to Raguel. "Lucas needs help."

Raguel rolled his eyes. "Doesn't he always."

I sighed. "No, he really needs your help. I tried to stint the blood, but I think he might have lost too much." Sometime during my rambling, Raguel had rushed out of the security room and up to my bedroom. I turned to follow.

Grief grabbed my heart threatening to pull it right out of my chest as I caught a glimpse of Lucas's black suit being carried off for cleaning.

Yesterday was the funeral. I couldn't cry as they lowered Eli's and Evie's empty caskets full of trinkets and dreams into the ground. Mine were in the casket with theirs.

Their parents had decided to proceed with funeral arrangements. Four months had been too long. They had lost hope that their children would return to them. I stood and stared blankly while everyone sobbed. I watched as their mother fell to her knees screaming with her pain. Their father sunk down with her on the ground holding her as his own violent sobs wracked through him.

I threw my newly purchased black dress away afterwards. I didn't want the reminder of the fact that they were gone. I felt the emptiness in my chest as vacant as an atramentous catacomb beneath the earth.

I finally had made it, panting to my bedroom door, when Raguel was just sitting down at the foot of the bed talking with a then awake Lucas.

I only caught snippets of their hushed and hurried conversation, something about the newscast. Lucas abruptly stood and rushed to change. He came out of my adjoining restroom and said to me, "We need to go to the security room." I gave him a look that should have conveyed my duh, but I no longer was sure if it did.

I followed Raguel and Lucas as they hurried to the security room. I, however, still breathless from my stint back up the stairs, chose to take the elevators.

The security room was pretty much a standard white room with a bank of large, wide-screen televisions, computers, and closed-circuit security video. On every single one of the TVs, destruction and mayhem were assaulting my senses.

Lucas stood slack-jawed at the screens, much like the rest of the room. I, however, was clueless. "What is going on?" I quizzed. Before anyone could respond, my face lit up the entire screen. And then it was my illuminating wings extending and the blast that damaged the buildings further. I cringed as the glass shattered and the already half-toppled building completely collapsed. Someone had recorded the incident from four months ago. Apparently, the footage had just now been released. The captions at the bottom of each screen read: "Angels among us?", "Spiritual warfare?" and "The end of the world is coming."

Someone unmuted one of the televisions. I stood openmouthed while the news anchor rambled on about angels causing destruction in the human world. At once, the TV was muted again, and everyone turned to stare at me.

I put my hands on my hips and sighed, "And so goes the digital age," as I sheepishly shrugged my shoulders, my cheeks the color of a ripened tomato. Raguel was about to go into one of his tirades when someone burst into the room with the shouts of, "We've found them."

My heart sank in my chest, a complete contradiction to their happy tone. It was time for me to go and bring back the bodies of the prophet and the law giver. Time for me to go and seek death.

<u>ACKNOWLEDGEMENTS:</u>

Acknowledgements are never easy. I wouldn't be where I am today without so many wonderful people.

First, I thank God for blessing me with everything that I have and everything that I am. Without him, I am nothing and have nothing. He hears my prayers. When I call, He answers. I wouldn't be who I am today if it were not for the infinite blessings, he's given me.

I'd like to also thank the best family support system a girl could ask for. Honestly, I don't know where I would be if it weren't for you all. Every single one of you.

My husband, my partner in everything, you were the one who helped me through it all. The house wouldn't be clean without you, the kids would never make it to school, and we'd never eat. You helped me through the worst of my inner doubts. You helped me fill the plot holes and fix story blunders. You encouraged me when I said, "I'm quitting, just wipe the hard drive." You held me through the tears. The late-night brainstorming marathons wouldn't be the same without your enthusiasm. I know there have been a few bad moments, but there have been extreme moments of joy. Like the day I finished the first chapter, the day I told everyone I was writing a book, the day I saw my name on my book cover and the day I finished writing it. Through it all, you've held my hand and at times the entirety of this book in yours. You knew I could do it before I did. I love you.

To my children, always have faith in yourself. Let this be proof of the great wonders you can achieve when you have faith. Thank you for the constant drink refills, snacks, "I love you mommy moments", the "how was writing today" questions, and the many, many, hugs and kisses along the way. You guys have helped me so much throughout this whole process, often never once knowing you were. Your excitement and encouragements have been overwhelming. I love you both more than you could possibly know.

To my parents, you both raised me not to be a "quitter" and trust me there truly were many times I thought about quitting. I even tried for a few years, but I just couldn't because I wasn't raised that way. You also raised me to believe in myself and taught us that hard work always pays off in the end. You've shown me what faith was and instilled in me your belief and trust in God. Thank you.

To my friends new and old, thank you for your kind and encouraging words of friendship and support. They mean more than you will ever know.

Megan, my best friend, thank you for lending me your eyes when I couldn't see my way out and your ears when I felt I had overburdened my husband. But thank you most of all for your Disney vacation temptations and sharing your sweet family.

My wonderful editor Carol Rushing, I've said it time and time again, Thank you from the bottom of my heart. You saw the hidden gem beneath the hard to understand phrases and the misspelled common words. We won't even discuss my hideous uses of punctuation. You have been so patient and encouraging to me during this entire process. I truly am grateful the Lord placed you in my path.

My fabulous cover artist, Regina Wamba at ReginaWamba.com, your cover has left me speechless, every single time I see it. You have a true gift. I am proud to be your soul sister. Thank you for your encouraging words and valiant support. I needed the kick in the rear end.

And lastly, let's not forget you dear readers. Thank you for letting me share my stories with you.

<h1 style="text-align:center"><u>About the Author:</u></h1>

Patricia D. Adams is a Christian, Wife and Mother of twin boys, or as she likes to call them "Twin Dragons". She lives in a small quiet town thirty miles south of Houston, Texas. She spends most of her days at home sporting T-shirts, P.J.'s and messy buns, under blankets with her dogs while creating worlds at the computer like a true introvert. When she's not at home, you can find her cheering on her boys as they play in the band and sing in the choir. She loves crafts, devours books like they are life, enjoys watching T.V. and Movies, fantasizes about ice cream, eats way too many Starburst, wins family board game night and her favorite color is purple. She is also extremely socially awkward, a Disney addict, Caffeine enthusiast, Libra, Ravenclaw, and a huge fan of the Winchester brothers. An ideal day for her would be spending time with friends and family, or possibly going to Disney World, she can't decide. Patricia D. Adams is the author of the Patriarchs Covenant Saga, A Young Adult four book series. A Secret Place of Thunder is her debut novel.

Find out more about the author and what's next at:

www.patriciadadams.com

Twitter: https://twitter.com/patriciadadams

Facebook: https://www.facebook.com/patriciadadamsbooks

Instagram: https://www.instagram.com/patriciadadams

Goodreads: https://www.goodreads.com/PatriciaDAdams-Author

Amazon: http://www.amazon.com/Patricia-Adams

Pinterest: https://www.pinterest.com/patriciaadams

Reddit: https://www.reddit.com/PatriciaAdams-Author

Tumblr: http://patriciaadamsauthor.tumblr.com/

Email: patriciadadams@hotmail.com00200